Beyond a Moment

Darrell Peter Borza

PublishAmerica
Baltimore

© 2007 by Darrell Peter Borza.
All rights reserved. No part of this book may be reproduced, stored in a retrieval system or transmitted in any form or by any means without the prior written permission of the publishers, except by a reviewer who may quote brief passages in a review to be printed in a newspaper, magazine or journal.

First printing

All characters in this book are fictitious, and any resemblance to real persons, living or dead, is coincidental.

ISBN: 1-4241-8232-8
PUBLISHED BY PUBLISHAMERICA, LLLP
www.publishamerica.com
Baltimore

Printed in the United States of America

CONTENT

Prologue	5
Chapter One: Looking Past the Moment	9
Chapter Two: What's Next?	17
Chapter Three: Walk with Me, Talk with Me	24
Chapter Four: Keeping It Real	36
Chapter Five: Finding America	50
Chapter Six: Eyes in the Sky	60
Chapter Seven: Pivotal Moments	69
Chapter Eight: Logistics of Spirit	75
Chapter Nine: Healing	82
Chapter Ten: Questions, Always the Questions	91
Chapter Eleven: Surreal Landscapes of the Mind	102
Chapter Twelve: The Elders	107
Chapter Thirteen: Hell Unleashed	117
Chapter Fourteen: Amazing, Just Amazing	129
Chapter Fifteen: Salvation	139
Chapter Sixteen: The Desert Keeps Her Secrets	154
Chapter Seventeen: Death Is Not the End	164
Chapter Eighteen: Desert Dreams	177
Chapter Nineteen: Goodbyes	190

Prologue

After leaving the coffee shop that day, my life was never to be the same again, not that I had an ordinary life to begin with. I had been shaken to the core of by spiritual beliefs and sensed it was a good thing. Every now and again we need to have our beliefs challenged, sort out the dead ones.

Some years ago I had abandoned teaching my meditation classes at the local spiritual centers. I was at odds with most of the centers and could not say why. Something about the whole spiritual movement had gone sour in my mind and it had been growing in me for quite a while.

In a few short weeks I had given away a collection of books it had taken me decades to accumulate on a wide variety of spiritually related subjects, covering centuries of time, from the newest to the ancient. I had become very alert to the need for something new and fresh in my pursuit of fulfillment. I suppose it came from the core realization that after decades of reading, research and practices, the goal still seemed to elude me.

I thought back of the people I knew when I began my infamous "journey "and how they were in the present.

Seemed to me that they were as unhappy, sickly, and disgruntled as they ever were then. A harsh judgment, perhaps, but a truthful observation nonetheless. I had made a lot of progress over the years, yet I still felt I was missing something as though I had all the pieces to this puzzle, but it needed to be assembled somehow.

I began to look for the common denominator to the people I was teaching, and although everyone was different unto themselves, their reasons for entering into spiritual education was a common one, they were miserable in their own lives, the same reason that spurred me into change. They had run out of reasons and people to blame for their unhappiness, so it was time for the great journey inward. "AAAhhh-UMMM."

Childhood abuses had set the stage for my self education, as it did for so many I had met. Each abuse case is real, pertinent to one's life direction and the reason for so many to remain stuck in misery most all of their lives.

Meditation, yoga, tai chi, even the new law of attraction craze will not take you to a life of bliss, joy, and prosperity, only I can do that, as in the infamous "I" can. The best spiritual, scientific, and metaphysical practices are tools, all the information in the universe will not help you without it coursing through you, and you alone. Most abused people have had some psychological counseling of one form or another, taking you to survival recognition "I am a survivor" mode, but the yearning to live a life far beyond it kicks in, then the real searching begins.

In my time I could not help but notice how the journey inward took so much outward reading, research, and how many people outside of us know the "way" for us. I have read a library of books which is a beautiful excursion into another's mind and thoughts, but not my own. The search inward now has many people watching galaxies for salvation of themselves.

I think going into ourselves is a scary place to travel. We head in with such negative preconceived notions of ourselves. Only to discover we are not so bad at all. Many of us have done things we are not proud of, wish we had not, even broken some serious laws, yet there is nothing that cannot be forgiven, and nothing we cannot set back into alignment.

In my conversation with the young woman from the coffee shop, we talked of this being the time of fruition of the practices that came before, the ones which had evolved across time since the days of the beginning, the old Schools of Mystery and the ancient sciences. We have focused so long on evolving ourselves we have not noticed that the arts themselves have evolved. The Earth is being bombarded at present by new energies into her atmosphere. These energies are allowing a quickening in our evolutions, and ability for meditation to achieve deeper levels in our energy selves, prayer to become a profound avenue of healing and accomplishment of goals.

The most profound change will be in the ways that we perceive being "only human" a phrase that in the past has excused our flaws, while the new present will see it defining the wonder of us, our ability to find our balance on any surface, in any situation.

We have become lost on "the Path" that promised to save us, bring us to fruition and make our lives a divine experience while on Earth, addicted to the struggle of attaining, chasing the carrot of enlightenment. The road less traveled now appears to be as the temple Jesus trashed, in mall form. It's all for sale by the prophets, gurus, and anyone that channels from the divine source in another more famous name. It is all assumed to be absolute truth when the name of Michael is attached to it, or some other dead saint who cannot sue you for using their names.

We are not as gullible as marketers presume us, nor as desperate for healing as the New Age has us convinced of, because we are not that diseased. Just as the pharmaceutical companies would have us believe via their commercials we are "suffering" from their diseases, so too the New Age has us convinced we are fundamentally flawed as religion proclaimed us to be, and cannot achieve divine status without their services.

Just as it takes twelve years of public schooling to produce another "worker human" it took eons of degradation education to convince the human race of its hopelessness and need of salvation.

But, it only takes one moment of abuse to change a human being for the entire duration of their life, one episode of molestation. My spiritual friends have always told me to "let it go" and I agree. Most people want to see abuse in all forms purged from human life, can it happen? Yes it can, in my belief and the belief of many others, when we begin to address the actual cause.

Let's start at the beginning, creation, and the idea that Source ever created an evolving being that was so flawed and so predatory. Believe what you will, but it makes no sense for this to have occurred. Yet history is what it is, and truth often disturbs our preferred beliefs. There are our ancestors that accomplished amazing things, and those that ate their young, again, it is what it was. So what is the truth here, are we the product of divine perfected being, or the result of primal brutality evolved? I feel it is like the theories of Creationism and Evolution. At first look they are opposing ideas, but let your mind blend them, the truth begins to unfold, one only needs to purge the need to be "right" in their ideal.

For a person from an abusive background to even conceive the idea of a world without abuse is in itself inconceivable. In my youth I viewed, as so many do, the best I could hope for was to become stronger than the energies that plague us, then as I grew and moved on in life, it evolved to a thought of just becoming an energy that repelled those that desired to do harm, then finally to putting no focus at all on the abusive energies.

That's when things started to cruise.

That is the path that led to what I witnessed in the coffee shop that day. The ability to create a human being that is stronger than all the aggressive energies in life. Strong enough to be loving and forgiving enough to release energies that do not belong to them back to whom it does, and stay free of the energies that bring them to a lower frequency. As long as we carry dark energies of dark experiences within us, we will continue to draw it to us. We can retain the memories of the ancient barbarian, but we do not need to carry the passion of it.

I
Looking Past the Moment

I sat at the local coffee shop, sipping an extremely overpriced cup of latte whose name had so many words I forgot them all. Before me lay a newspaper I placed there for effect alone, disguising my favorite pastime of people watching.

In these times being psychic is not a thing of uniqueness, and it puts a whole new twist into people watching, as I am not seeking to know people's secrets but to know those that are aware I am sensing them. It is easy to "feel" a person as their energy passes my own, people do this unconsciously all the time. My eyes and senses kept drifting to a young woman in the corner booth just staring into her coffee cup as if reading her fortune in the grounds. She looked up and met my eyes, then turned her attention to the counter and the line of addicts that gathered here daily, like myself.

Actually I rarely come here, as I prefer my own coffee, but awoke early with a sense I needed to go out and be amongst the living this morning. I have been doing this long enough to follow my hunches and inspirations.

My senses were on high alert, which generally meant that something or someone was going to appear in my life today for a reason.

The girl was the reason I was sensing. She appeared to be rather young to be here so early, perhaps fifteen or sixteen, yet with a face reflecting maturity far beyond the years of her body, this girl had known suffering. Yet the field of energy surrounding her was reflecting colors of an enlightened person with educated wisdom of the spiritual kind. She was short with shortly cropped brown hair, green eyes and a sense of purpose for her presence in this place. She kept glancing between the counter, to me, and back to her cup. She was awaiting the arrival of someone. I used my senses to try and scan her, but she was blocking any such intrusion, but was aware there was "like mind" in the room. This was proving to be intriguing and I was glad I dragged myself here, but didn't know why yet.

The stream of people went along in what appeared to be a routine for both customer and employees, with the usual and customary grunts of "good morning" and "have a nice day" monologues. I noticed the girl looking up with every new arrival and felt surges of her energy with each new arrival. It was difficult pinpointing the nature of it though, fear, anticipation, a lover perhaps. But, to be certain it was an intense thought behind its power.

I returned to my coffee and pretend newspaper reading.

I was suddenly jarred out of my thoughts, I felt a darkness enter the shop, like a storm cloud amongst the light and pure ones. A tall elderly man in his sixties entered and approached the counter, he was smiling as he ordered.

His length of time talking to the counter person indicated a multiple order, amidst mindless chitchat from both.

He was balding with bushy eyebrows and emanated an energy in direct contradiction to his smile and stance, this was a practiced demeanor, one that thought and controlled energy was put into to create a mask of self.

My eyes turned towards the girl, her eyes were directed at him, and had become steeled in their expression, unblinking and immovable from him. Her energies were undulating now from head to toe, and growing darker with each wave, it was as if I were watching a tsunami building. This was her awaited destination and it was no lover and no friend she was here to meet, this was something I had never felt or witnessed in forty years of energy work and experience. I was here to witness something new.

I attempted to probe her emotion and was literally propelled back again, as if I had been thrown against the wall by a punch. My breath was stilled by its power and intensity. My eyes snapped to the object of her laser stare.

I could plainly see he was feeling it, but was engrossed in his task. It was affecting him as a mosquito buzzing his space, subtle twitching and hand gestures of irritation were appearing. I was in awe that the others were not feeling any of this, but closer scrutiny revealed people were actually moving away from him unconsciously, even walking out his way to get to the counter. It was a subtle play being performed, but the dramatic conclusion was not far off in time and space. Whatever this was going on here, it was definitely "show time" here and now.

I moved my position to be able to see them both unencumbered, resigning myself to the role of observer, and being put in my place by a quick snap of the girl's eyes to me as I moved. I actually heard her in my mind "stay out of this" and I relayed to her "I shall" without a conscious formation of the thought. This was being played out in an arena of energies I was not yet familiar in, and that I doubted many on this planet had. Yet I felt somehow privileged to be a witness to it.

I could see her energies as clearly as I could the seat she was sitting in. A stream of white gold light was entering her crown, her body was enveloped in a white light aura, but from her root came a black energy up through her body, circling in the heart chakra, and moving up to her third eye. The darker energies were lines like lasers through the rest, and it was shooting from her directly into the old man's heart chakra. Her eyes revealed nothing of what was transpiring nor her body. She appeared to be just a young woman sitting here staring into the nothingness we all see from time to time, lost in thought we call it.

The man was very uncomfortable now, sweating and moving in what appeared small convulsionary motions, trying desperately to hide his discomfort. His practiced mode was beginning to breakdown under the stress he was feeling. Others around him were widening the girth as when someone is having a stroke or heart attack. The sense tells us to move away for something very personal is occurring. He was looking around for a source of this discomfort, for even unto the end, we seek outside before resigning ourselves to the reality it is within. It is always within.

Then his eyes saw her, and the locking was inseparable, they were one now. The flow from her reached light speed and beyond in the connection, and on his lips was a grin that sent shivers into my being, too large to be contained in the spine. This man was her molester of many years, the thief of her innocence and the torturer of her mind. I had to look away to calm the nausea in my stomach and the revulsion in my mind.

I looked again at her, and there were seven orbs of light around her head now, with streams aligned to her crown, they were the others he had hurt. I knew this to be the truth of it. The lasers within her were becoming lighter, as the aura of the old man became a swamp of muddy, murky anguish. He could take no more, he screamed in pain as his face twisted and contorted in torturous fury, he fell to the ground clutching his chest as onlookers stood frozen to the tiles. In one last cry of eternal pain, he went silent as the bloodcurdling scream echoed in everyone's mind, filling the little shop like wind unable to escape. He lay dead, twisted and frozen in a horrible contortion that would awaken each bystander for weeks in their sleep.

I looked at the girl, and saw consciousness returning her reality in her eyes, she turned and looked again into her coffee, a tear forming in her eye. Her aura was pure white, calm and serene, with specks of old and blue appearing and disappearing within its purity. She looked over at me, our eyes locked, fear knee jerked into my consciousness. Words form her mind flowed into mine. "Be at peace, as I am and the old man too."

I walked over to her and sat down. We did not speak as the rest unfolded. The police screaming up with paramedics arriving, people yelling and crying, some running away in confusion and panic. I overheard the paramedic say to the police it was an obvious stroke or heart attack, or both, accounting for the contorted position of the man and the grimace look frozen on his face. We sat there for hours in total silence until all was as it had been before this event. Even the manager had calmed down from the panic he thought would ensue from someone dying in his little coffee shop.

We left the shop together and walked to a park close by. There we talked until night enveloped us and we went our separate ways. I was bound to never repeat our conversation, as it was one of newly defined personal nature.

She asked me to keep our words a secret, and I gave her my oath to do so, but charged me to explain the nature and purpose of this day's newly evolved ability of human exchange.

Did she murder that man? I thought so while in the coffee shop, so would the police if they saw what my eyes and senses did, but they could not. I accused her of it at the onset of our talk later. Looked like murder by controlled energy to me.

Yet, I was wrong in my observation, and would soon learn why, and much more. She and others had been molested by this man, teacher for many years, under a threat of hurting their families if they ever revealed it to anyone, even to the degree of having stalked and photographed their families to ensure his access to them all.

Not so uncommon in circles of twisted humans, and one a child lives in deathly fear of, it is torture over years.

She told me what I was observing and it was not revenge, nor was his death anything but his own choice within the experience, he did not have to die, but chose to. It was not an act of anger or hatred, but one of self purification and self love of herself. It was an act of self-salvation.

What I was witnessing in the matrix of her energy was a large part of the chakras purpose within us, as we have always viewed them as processing centers for our incoming energies, but they also aid us in the control of energy we emit from us. Our five senses also can emit energy and sensation as well as take them in. We are designed to work both ways in all of our design.

She too had awakened that morning earlier than usual and felt compelled to visit the coffee shop which was not her custom, but she followed her intuitions, that she was very accustomed to doing, as most abused people are.

For within the experiences of abuse, quantum evolutions are taking place of biology and mental abilities, and the results can be the same as that of a lifetime of spiritual practices. This girl was given many hats to wear in her young life by the powers that controlled her. In spiritual circles she was called Indigo or Crystal child. At school she was called anti-social by administrators, and freak by the students. At home she was called a lot of things, but few of them complimentary.

She had taught herself to meditate, read books on spiritual practices, science books on quantum physics, and related biologies and psychotherapies. She fed her mind with a veracious appetite for knowledge, for knowledge was power, and power would free her from her prison. During abuse she was a master at out-of-body experience and left.

But things have changed a lot in the universe and in evolution of the human race. Under the noses of life's busy commerce and self-indulgent people, a new species has evolved into our midst. For centuries we have talked of this evolutionary path, often referring to it as "the Path" but never seeing that someday it would be our reality.

Like the prophet so busy writing it, he fails to see it is occurring in his midst.

BEYOND THE MOMENT

What occurred that day was a returning to the old man that which was his alone, she returned to him all the emotions he had left in her, imprinted onto her, and branded into her mind, the feelings of fear filled dread that were never hers to hold and to keep. In that laser beam of emotion, she was simply giving him back what he had so uncaringly left for her to deal with, leaving her as he had originally found her, her innocence unburied and pure of the sludge of his desires gone mad. For one cannot lose their innocence, just misplace it in the darkness.

When all that he had caused her to feel returned to his mind, it was more than he could bear. More than he had ever taken the time to consider, and the horrible anguish was more than he could live with, so he chose not to live anymore, and in his last conscious moment he heard he was truly forgiven. Yet chose to leave, so she was a carrier of no guilt or remorse, no crime had been committed.

She explained to me and to herself that this was the way of it now, and that the human race would now see the truth of justice and be guided into right action and thinking along this road of returning feelings to their proper owners. It was the way of the ones that came before her, called saints, messiahs, and divine, but now it is the way of us all. That DNA had a new code and new energy field of highly evolved codes emitting from them, they formed sacred geometries of perfected design. Allowing what we had been witness to this morning. This is what used to refer to in death as "our life passing before our eyes" seeing by feeling how we had made every person in our life feel in our interaction with them. Returning to them the product of their thoughts and emotion towards us.

Yet death need not be the catalyst for this revelation any longer. This also allows us to show in very real ways appreciation of the love and the kindness we have been given, the matrix sends equal and infinite love from eye to eye as in the coffee shop.

It has been four years since that day, and we have not spoken eye to eye since that day. She will be graduating college soon as a counselor to abused people, doing as she said that day she would, to teach and awaken everyone she could to this within themselves, and to connect with those awakened by their own experiences as she was. There is a "new sheriff" in planet earth, making all the others obsolete.

She asked me to write a book of all this, and this is the forerunner to it. She is out there somewhere and everywhere, and she looks like many young women and men, so be careful what you leave in the life of others. It will be returned to you, because it belongs to you.

II
What's Next?

I didn't think about the coffee shop the whole way up to her graduation, I had vowed not to. I wanted to arrive at the graduation ceremony focused and clear. I meditated most of the two-hour drive, talked to myself, and blasted some excellent music.

Over the last five years the young woman and I had written, emailed, and talked sometimes. Sometimes we talked in silence, as we had been for the last twenty minutes of my arrival. She had been in her senior year of high school when we met and today was graduating college. Never had we talked of that morning in the coffee shop, the old man, and our subsequent all-night talk. Neither of us could ever discover a need to.

When you step through the veil, there is no reason to look back at the door, because you truly realize at that point there never was one.

The college was tucked away in the Ohio countryside, where peace was commonplace and stars and the moon lit the night as one would expect in a quiet country town. Scholarships and summer remote work programs fed her academic endeavors, while tours in the South American jungles fed her spirit and strengthened her body. Still short cropped dark hair, green almond-shaped eyes still seeking and sending. It was a feeling of one flow appearing to be multidimensional for the observers in life. But, aren't we all? Humans fight hard for their restriction while protesting it at the same time.

Our faces had been burned into each other's memories so deeply and detailed it was there for future generations to observe at will. During our first talk, more sensory communication occurred than verbal. So it was easy to visualize her face in meditation and connect, and doing so was becoming easier and easier. Such ability is not the advantage of a few, everyone is designed for total communication by biological design and mind ability. It is a feeling, because feeling is the universal language, the true divine syntax of communication into the larger mind of ourselves, the world and the universe itself.

Onward and upward to the ceremony. I felt every past life that had attended one of these yawns. Tradition has its place and it is difficult to inject newness into it. I think the same speeches have been traditionally handed down from school to school, honor student to honor student.

Although, the most unique one I have ever heard was at my high school graduation. The person delivering it was a young woman I had attended catholic school with in our younger years. She was extremely smart and very genuinely nice, caring and sincere. If she asked how your day was, she was sincerely interested in the answer.

In her speech she essentially cold-cocked the class and administration for the way that she had been treated by the students for being smarter than most of the teachers and the administration for closing their eyes to the torment of a lot of the student body, while focusing on the those that played sports, cheerleaded and their rich parents. They didn't see it coming and Bernadine did not advertise her speech beforehand. They just assumed she would deliver a speech about the "good old days" of high school and world peace. They could not have been more wrong. The speech was followed by thunderous applause and cheering and at least two-thirds of the graduation leaving behind Bernadine's exit from the stage. Ah, the good old days.

I had hoped for the same today, a hopeful break from the mundane rhetoric of these events, a spark of new boldness in the youth heading out into the world. I took a seat in the warm sun and patiently awaited the festivities.

I suppose it is time to give this young woman a name for reading purposes. I only know her by her screen name "Self Messiah," as introductions escaped us when we met. They somehow seemed to fall into the category of unimportant considering the morning's events. I scanned the graduate name list in the booklet, seeing if I could sense her name. I felt a psychic tap on my mind's eye. "Sarah" I heard sweep into my mind — "Got it, thanks."

I spotted her in the sea of swaying robes across the grass waiting for a line to form into the seats. She was a thousand miles away in her expression, and I was sensing the impatience to be past this afternoon. I drifted off into a mantra I used for just such occasions. "God, wake me when it's over" repeated in old Vedic tradition of course. At last her row began to move. I thought she was beginning the receiving portion of the show, but she was going to give a speech, odd a whole row mobilizing for it though.

As the row moved across the grass to the stage, they fanned out in a V formation, like geese flowing into position for flight, with Sarah at point, this was deliberate for effect. They have my attention.

As the wind blew their robes, I was swept into a glimpse of a future scene of robed people ascending to a new order of life, feeling I had read it in a book that was not yet written, but in the works.

She walked directly to the podium and began to speak as the others formed a half circle behind her, ten people in all, six women and four men.

"Our youth is trapped, in the diaphragm of the world's breathing. We are being squeezed by the in-breath of the old, and uncaringly thrown into a void as the new breathes out into life. This is more than the natural order of breathing, this is the last breath of this world as we know it.

"One has only to observe their own lives to see this is so. Search your own hearts for truth, see what you are looking at. Then go to a mirror to find the answers you seek, they lie nowhere else.

"When I arrived here at college, I was grown far beyond my years. I had learned that learning never ceases, choose to stop learning and death begins. So, my fellow students, be students forever into time, and be masters in the moment. This is how we escape the breathing of humankind and become the embodiment of the breath. We are the new breath of life into life.

"These people behind me are those I taught when I arrived. They in turn have taught hundreds more, and those hundreds are teaching thousands. Teaching what? A simple technique for ridding ourselves of the toxins that preceded us, the ones we were born into and became infected with through experiences of Neanderthals still walking amongst us. You will know who you are before this speech concludes, as a demonstration will soon follow of what we bring to life. This may well be the most unique graduation in history.

"Under the cloak of greed, corruptions, and war for the sake of genetic cleansings and profit, the old species of human perception has reigned. Now, a new species of human erectus has appeared, unnoticed, unfettered and uncontrollable. We are a species within a species, neither superior or inferior, just different."

I looked out across the audience, as "fight or flight" emotional instinct began to permeate the air. My God, it's the coffee shop on mass scale. This is going to get interesting to say the least. People were showing signs of an uneasiness they could not define, the worst kind for a human being. Some were even sitting on the edge of their seats in anticipation of what was following, although thoughts were flooding the area, none had caught the energy of this. So I returned to listening.

"Our economies are fear based," she continued. "At present, with illness, dysfunction, and disease as the sustaining economic monopoly that drives us. Simple observation dictates that the market cannot cure its customer base without killing their profits, so perpetuation is the banner in the subconscious of these businesses of human misery. Even our spiritual healers are not seeing what they look at in their client's eyes. Hope is the mass produced product of our times, the carrot that leads the horse blindly.

"From rural towns to leading cities of the world, people are being drained of their energies in all its forms. Governments, religions, businesses, even the spiritual movement have tapped the masses for what will sustain them. The rape of Earth includes the rape of its people. Yet blame lies only in one place, the place you are sitting, standing, or preparing to flee from. The plight of the masses lies on the shoulders of each person that makes up the mass of human life.

"The generation before you is here to say that it is not changing, but that it *has* changed. This generation has no focus on what was, even unto a moment ago. We have no desire to look for and resolve conspiracies, to punish those that exploit so many, nor to seek revenge on past horrors.

"We are here living now, without a thought of what was. This is what graduates this day into life from a sleepy country college in Ohio. Great speeches have gone before mine, mighty words of hope and promise for the world from its newest participants, yet life seems to droll on and on down the same road. The human race has yet to imagine a world and an economy based on wellness, wholeness of the human being, and what such a world would do. Today we embark on a new road, today we will know what that feels like and where it will lead us."

Sarah took two steps away from the podium and stood in the middle of the half circle of her fellow graduates. She closed her eyes and the others joined her in the silence. "Show time!"

I had moved out of my seat to gain an overall view of the people there. I was also connected to Sarah's emotions, and I felt a familiar stirring from deep within myself. My mind's eye saw what had occurred so many years ago in the coffee shop: charkas aligning, energy streamlining, third eyes preparing to laser out that which was not theirs, returning emotional feelings not belonging to themselves. This could get gruesome, I was thinking.

"Trust," I heard gently in my entire being.

So I trusted, and then I watched, listened, and joined. I saw as I had before, the energies in this woman flow from her outward to people in the audience, as well as the other ten. Streams going out into people they knew returning the toxic emotions they had left at their mind's door and the heart's plateaus. It was having similar effects as in the coffee shop, but somehow less intense, as the offenses were less I believe.

People the energy was directed at were affected deeply, tears flowed with cries of anguish from some, even men were crying from their emotions overwhelming them. All this took place in seconds as energy flowed from the people on stage into the directed people they were focusing upon.

Then something amazing occurred, after releasing the negative emotions, the line of energy being projected turned to a golden color and immediately engulfed these same people. This was the love these people on stage felt for the others, the gratitude and appreciation they harbored for them.

Tears flowed even harder with this revelation of projected ability of emotion. In their faces was a relief that they had prayed for now realized. They were able to clearly see how they had impacted the lives of many in a very positive and uplifting way, far outweighing any of the lower energies. As the love poured into them, not only did they feel forgiveness for their mistakes, but pure once again, as though they had never made any mistakes at all.

From start to finish, it was minutes in its length, yet light years of change had somehow occurred.
Sarah and the rest left the stage and returned to their seats. The ceremony resumed as scheduled as students began the receiving of their diplomas, like a robed river moving across the stage. There was a sense of urgency in the air to get through this part, because the dominating energy was one of unity in all the people here. The energy that was directed to individuals in a very intimate exchange was felt by everyone, the loving energy had spread through the crowd like water through a city street after a child opened the hydrant on a hot summer's day, nothing but relief and joy.
I saw where this was all heading in my mind's heart and my eyes saw something occurring that would sweep the face of the Earth like a tsunami without the preceding earthquake. It had to start somewhere, like the coffee shop that morning, and why not a sleepy Ohio college town?
As the ceremony came to a close, people were out their seats with the last few words, then there was a rush to each other I had not seen since once stupidly being at a mall the day after Thanksgiving at opening time. I meandered through the crowd casually just listening to bits an pieces of loved ones reuniting in the moment, and some after decades of separation in the same home. I overheard apologies, promises to leave there and talk, changes promised, and "I am sorry" like it was a mantra for the day.
Sarah had promised to spend the following day with me to reacquaint ourselves.
I returned to my motel room and let it all settle in.

III
Walk with Me, Talk with Me

We met at sunrise near the lake at the park where the graduation took place. It was a beautiful sunrise with the sky's colors making love to one another in a constantly changing undulation of passion and harmony.

I saw her coming down the hill across the finely trimmed lawn, her aura flowing behind her like the robe she wore yesterday. The sun was hitting her head on and it was a picture I would etch into my mind, like a person entering this dimension from some alien portal.

Her chakras were wide open, creating an energy field that felt impenetrable to anything known to humankind, and swept outward from her so far it seemed to be blending with the sky.

"Well that was quite a demonstration at your graduation yesterday," I said.

"Yes, it was designed to be. It's out there now, no turning back," she replied.

"Out there? Seems to me that once you make a public display like that, you're opening yourself up to a lot criticism. A lot of misunderstandings."

"That's old thinking. The difference now is that the energy precedes the action, if only by a nano-second. Once engulfed in the energy of it, belief evolves into undeniable reality of emotion, feeling supercedes knee jerk responses from fear. You know the feelings I speak of."

"I think your 'Neanderthal' reference was an offense to some."

"Facts are facts, and being politically correct doesn't stop reality, only attempts to control it. We both know that is not possible. The search for the common genetic link doesn't bear fruit because there is not one lineage but many. Many variations of humankind walk the planet from many originating lines."

"I would agree with that, and find political correctness amusing in a dark humor sort of way. I also know the line you walked to get here isn't relevant any longer."

"The very point of my demonstration at graduation."

"Yes, what was the 'point' exactly? I feel I know, but hearing you explain it would aid the ingestion I think."

"Ingestion indeed. God is the primitive terminology for energy, yet it remains sacred all through time. People are starving in countries where food is abundant just as ones that are poverty-stricken. After graduation I got calls from people we asked to report what occurred after they returned home. It was an amazing transition, the food was laid out, parties as usual. Yet most said everyone talked openly, forgave and asked forgiveness, fresh starts all across the board, so to speak."

"Ah yes, but don't fresh starts get spoiled when things realign to 'normal' again?"

"They can, often do, but this is a new time, a very new one. That alone was the point of yesterday. I recall a line from my studies: 'all will be revealed' and that is all this process does. Brings it to light, the truth of what is really felt, unto the giver and the receiver. The old man in the coffee shop had done much wrong to many, but it is not so for most people. They think they have done unforgivable acts, it blows up in their minds until they see it is not so grievous."

"So what is next from here? I felt the people in the audience yesterday walking away in dismay at their own feelings, most thinking it was the reality their little children were all grown now, and the feelings coming from their memories and fears of this day. I sense what truly occurred will not be realized for a while yet."

"Probably not, but does it matter? All that matters is the cleansing of everyone's toxic energy, you know that is the truth. You know what is happening here. The toxins being removed bring the light to life within them."

"Yes, I know this is true."

"I sense doubt."

"No, you sense a man that has been here before, seen hope like this wave into humanity for the last four decades, and seen most still living the same lives they did before. Each spiritual miracle that came down the pike, the 'newest' discoveries, processes, techniques. Yaddi—yaddi—yah. It is so old it has grown boring.

"Wow, that is some serious cynicism."

"No, just some serious caution. I agree what has occurred on our meeting is new, but not as new as one might think. In a way, this is the logical result of genetic evolution as well as spiritual evolvement. Sooner or later humanity had to come to realize that they were more than evolved apes, more than even their imaginations could conjure up."

"I agree, this was not possible even one generation ago. We had to evolve in a parallel lineage with the universe's evolution. All things had to come into alignment for this quantum leap to occur, and so it is now. I am hardly the only one in the world doing this."

"I suspected as much, after forty years of meditation, one cannot help but sense everywhere and connect with others in the same frequencies. Meditate long enough and you know you are millions in the meditation, past and present are there with you."

"Yes, and what we are doing here is the same, only we are doing it with our eyes wide open, our senses fully awake and far-reaching. Everything before this was the in-breath, now we breathe outward."

We walked awhile in silence, seemingly, to those walking about now. The beauty of the day was bringing many out now, nature is still the only true healer on the planet. Whatever the darkness in your mind, the sun will fill it with light and lighten your burdens.

We sat quietly from speech and in our minds. People were walking, playing, dogs ran in their freedom from leashes. A couple across the water were arguing, evident in the arm gestures that expressed total futility even as they continued arguing. Some people drank coffee to get going in the morning, some pumped their adrenaline with negative emotion as the primer.

"All right, time to ask the unanswered question. I understand your role, why am I here, why was I called to get coffee that morning and witness your purging?"

"You don't know?"

"Yes, I think I do, I just want your version of it."

"We have unfinished business you and I."

"Ah yes, unfinished business, seems to be the theme of my life this lifetime. Am I going to be a twisted heap on the floor too?"

"Only if you choose it to be as he did. I suspect you will not make that choice though. Why would you? We have a lot of work to do, if you choose that."

"This sort of work seems to choose the person. Yet in the final analysis somewhere in our life we asked for this. We asked what others were too afraid to ask, more specifically too afraid to find the answers to. We were the ones that had to look into the darkness and see what was here."

"Yes, we are the ancestors of the ones that slipped away from the caves in the darkness of night, plotting our course through the darkness while foraging during the day. Every day we would take a step farther into the forbidden zones. Then one night we walked away, never to be seen again, becoming the stories they told later children to keep them in the cave at night also. Where did we go?"

"In my youth we were the 'black sheep' another politically

incorrect term by now I am sure. The ones that just couldn't seem to stay with the 'program' mainly because our childhood experiences were truth behind the normal bullshit screen. Another tragic tale of wasted youth."

"Mine too, but we owe our abuse our evolvement. Had I not been molested, I would have had a normal childhood, and not ever read, studied and applied it, but I am here to tell everyone 'those days are over' and to show them the new days are dawning."

"And how's that working out for you?"

"Let's take a walk into town and I will show you how it is working."

"And our unfinished business?"

"It's waited three millennium, a few more hours won't hurt."

We headed off towards town, along a path leading from the park lined with ancient maple trees in full bloom, their arching limbs forming a natural tunnel. I am sure this was a favorite lane for lovers to walk, young and old.

I think the same architect designed every college town in America, imported the same kids, pizza places. Hundreds of young people walking briskly with back packs slung behind them, all looking the same to achieve difference somehow. I love it.

Everyone we passed seemed to know Sarah. She would stop frequently to speak to people as I just let my eyes take it all in, and introduced myself as her uncle twice removed from a previous marriage between two of her close cousins. Oddly enough they seemed to be OK with it. So many people spoke to her, conversation was not desired as we walked. In our minds there was a constant flow though, not language, sentences, paragraphs, but more of a sharing being conveyed in a stream of energy. It is hard to articulate the idea as it does not pay attention to time or space, past and present can and are being related as a current event regardless of the time line.

BEYOND THE MOMENT

In the mind's ability to communicate this way, we could take a segment of history from Egypt and apply it to the present changes, as both source and outcome, seeing a lineage of then into now of an ideal began when Pharos walked their palace gardens. Even speaking in silence of the plans from Hathor's female Pharos being culminated on the stage yesterday morning by a twenty-year-old woman in this century, discussing all of history of this new era as one day in time.

"Where are we going?" I asked her.

"To a spiritual center we started in town."

"Wow, how original. Let me guess, gems and crystals, rows of books on everything remotely spiritual, handmade crafts from Taiwan, and of course, scented candles for aromatherapy. Lest we not forget 'Madame Zelda' doing psychic readings for the love lost and tea leaf reading for the more serious student of the occult."

"Does someone need a nap?"

"Sorry, that cynicism again. Arises every time I smell incense while hearing Enya across from two people passing a joint that will help me see God."

"Forget the nap, you need to be bitch slapped."

"Bring it on, you're short I can take you."

"Yes, well you're old."

"Had to go there, didn't you? OK enough, let's get back to adulthood shall we. So what makes this spiritual store different from the others? I mean the spiritual movement is now the spiritual market. Every time I walk into one I feel like Jesus at the temple the day he trashed it. In fact I get very clear imagery of it happening."

"Yes, me too. I get the same imagery when I walk into a Christian church anymore. My best friend growing up was a born-again Christian, at least her parents were. We would study together at night, meditation, we did yoga and studied the old manuscripts of Tibetan knowledge. Over the course of

29

our childhood we studied everything we could read, the sciences too. She now runs the center."

"OK, but again, what makes it unique?"

"I wouldn't say unique, I would say new, in its purpose more so than its layout. Ironically it is in an old cathedral in town, just a few blocks up now. It was a Congregationalist church, the architecture is amazing. Old-world windows of stained glass, beams two feet thick, very 'freemason' looking and feeling. I loved the building the first time I saw it from the bus window when I arrived."

"Sounds awesome, I can't wait to see it. I grew up Catholic, so the old cathedrals still make me feel at home in a nostalgic sort of way, but not near God at all, as I pointed out to a priest once. 'God' is such a small word for what I feel and believe anymore, what I know to be the vastness of it all. I cannot be comfortable in the old terminologies any longer, any of it, even the ways and practices of the past that have brought us here to this moment."

"I agree with that totally, which is why we are here talking now. The center is just around the corner."

As we rounded the corner we could hear people talking, no, it was praying in unison. What the hell is this? I wondered. There was at least thirty people in front of the place praying and moving in a circle so typical of protesters. They were Christians from the local Baptist church, each wearing a pin of identification as "God's soldiers" apparently here to fight the soldiers of Satan's New Age army. It took my mind a few seconds to wrap around the scene as being real, but it was. I looked over at Sarah to see if this was common place or a new phenomenon since yesterday. Her jaw on the pavement said it was definitely new.

I looked back at the protesters trying to sense what they were actually protesting, all I could feel was fear, angry fear. My instinct was to grab Sarah's arm and move her out of sight, but this wasn't my town, my center or my show, it was hers.

"Well, I didn't see this coming," she said in a whisper.
"You can't see everything, surprises are cool, keeps us on our toes."
"Well, what to do, what to do. I am going to address them directly."
"I wouldn't miss this for the world."
"Me either."
She walked up the steps of the old cathedral, seven in all and came to rest beneath the great arch of the doors, arched oak doors that radiated their ancient regal ness stood directly behind her, dwarfing her small framed body even more. Yet she began to radiate an energy that seemed to be having a direct impact on the anger of these people. The circle slowed as they began to focus on her, a woman in her fifties took the lead, obviously the leader of this time warp into religious intolerance.
"I was there yesterday, I saw what you did!" she screeched at Sarah. "You are Satan's spawn, daughter of evil! You have taken God's church and turned it to your headquarters of the devil's work."
Are you kidding me, who talks like that anymore? The insanity played on. I saw no fear in Sarah's eyes or her demeanor, just a quiet patience as the woman vomited her fears on the walk and the wind blew them away. She rambled on for ten minutes reciting scriptures, waving her hands in fits of frustrated rage, and finally fell silent. It felt like an ill wind had moved off freeing sunlight in the wake of silence.
"What do you think I did yesterday?" Sarah asked quietly.
"You know what you did, you whore of hell!"
"I am no whore, nor do I work for Satan. I do not believe in Satan."
I began to talk to Sarah mind to mind. "Wrong answer for this crowd," I sent her. "This is a very fundamentalist fanatic, she is going to take you out if she can, she is just looking for a way to defend it."

"I know," I heard her saying, "watch the man behind her please. He has a gun in his pocket. The tall one that is not moving at all."

"I am aware of that, and he is dying to use it for God."

"I am going with the truth here."

"That should do it, are looking to get shot?"

"No, of course not, but this needs to play out, don't you feel it?"

"Not what I am focusing on at the moment! That guy is going to shoot you, he wants to so badly he can taste it."

I moved in closer to try and get into the man's reach, but others blocked me. This was thought out before they arrived, this wasn't a protest, it was an assassination.

"You know they are here to kill you?"

"I do now!"

"Let's call for some help here then."

We both focused on calling out to those that could read us. People working in the center began to come out of the doors and surround Sarah. From both sides of the street and behind me, people were coming across the grass and moving toward the protesters.

The man with the gun began to look frustrated and nervous, he had no clear way to accomplish his goal anymore, there were just too many people around him and Sarah to make a move. I thought Sarah would seize this moment to slip inside to safety, but she didn't. She moved in front of those around her and began to speak to the people there.

"Stop this, now!" she commanded. "Stop it. There is no need for any of this, no reason for all this fear."

She turned to the people behind her and spoke to them for a few moments and then turned back to the people that had come to protest. The others seemed to go silent behind her and were obviously focusing on calm and sending out energies to change the overall mood of the situation. I moved up a few steps and stood off to her side to be closer to her, and stayed within a few feet of the man.

"This is not going to accomplish anyone's goals or desires for today or in the long run. All this will do is prolong everyone's unhappiness and fear. You, the man with the gun in your pocket, what do you think killing anyone will do? Do you believe that your faith asks you to shoot people as a solution to your imagined threats? Has killing doctors in the name of God stopped abortion, or even slowed them down? Quite the contrary, it only fuels the desire for more, to press the issue more and more into society and create more and more clinics."

"God hates you!" It was the woman that was yelling initially.

"No! God does not hate. How could you be a woman of God and even think such a thought about your God? How can you be a Christian and even have hate in your vocabulary? This is fear, fear of what you do not know and understand, what is new and been judged as evil in its newness. I know I am not going to change your minds here, but I am not going to stand here and be shot for reasons even you do not believe in your hearts."

She pointed then to the man, and asked, "What are you going to do now?"

He was looking to the ground, obviously lost in the turn around of this event. He had removed his hand from his pocket, cognizant of the reality his plan was done for now. The expression on his face had gone from anger, to bewilderment, now settling into awkwardness.

If he thought he could run, he would, but now with a finger pointing at him, he is frozen in time until he musters a response of some kind.

"I didn't come here to shoot you, I came to protect my mother."

"Protect her from what?" Sarah demanded.

"From you, this place and your beliefs."

"What are my beliefs?" she demanded again.

"Since you opened this place, a lot of people have stopped coming to church. They are coming here, listening to you tell them New Age lies, teaching them they can be like God. They come here and abandon the true God. You are the enemy of God to teach such things. We have sent people here to listen to what you tell them. We have sent people here to see what you are about. You teach blasphemy and the devil's ideas."

"What do you believe?"

"I believe in God, the true God, and that no one can be like God. It is evil to think you can, to even put yourself on that level. Jesus was the only Son of God. The only one that was ever like God, with God. What you teach is heresy, evil, and wrong. I was at the graduation, I saw the spell you put on people, I saw the devil in action there."

"No, you saw people feeling, exchanging the truth of what they felt and being better for it. They forgave and asked forgiveness, then moved past the past, and into the feeling they felt in the present, they loved one another. Is this not the very teachings of Jesus?"

"Do not presume to know the teachings of Jesus. You are not a Christian, you do not go to church and you do not believe the truth."

"I DO know the teachings of Jesus, I DO presume to know him, I Do live them, and the graduation ceremony lived them to the letter of them."

"No you do not. You teach here things that make people believe they are God. The Bible speaks of those like you in these times, the end times. People with words that promise and do not deliver, swaying others from the truth."

"That gun in your pocket, what teaching and truth does that come from? What teaching of Jesus does that prove? What commandment does it honor? Are you a man of God, or just another fanatic breaking your own religious beliefs to prove your righteousness?"

"Word games, you are playing mind games."

"No, I am playing no game at all."

Sarah walked down the steps toward the man, right past the woman, his mother, while she glared hatred at her as intensely as she could. Sarah glanced her way, in an instant returned her emotions to her, causing her to stumble backwards into the arms of others there. She walked up to the man and looked at him, never taking her eyes from his. She reached into his pocket and took the gun out, he moved no muscle to stop her. She took his left hand and placed the gun in his palm, and took the other hand bringing it up to the gun as well. She then released the safety, cocked it, and brought the barrel to her heart, still while locking eyes with him.

"If you really believe what you're saying, then shoot."

IV
Keeping It Real

Here we are, the moment of truth, to shoot or not to shoot, this is the question. There they stood, gun in hand and her heart pressed to the barrel. I scanned those on the steps, not a worry in their faces, they were still and calm. While the protesters were widening the circle of this event, some considering running, as they had not signed up for something this dramatic, just a peaceful protest against New Age contamination of their city. When you side with unbendable and inadaptable dogma it can never end well. Sarah was still staring into his eyes. I sensed a dialogue between them, and it is bad psychic manners to intrude.

I sensed no fear in Sarah at all, only intensity of purpose, while the man was frozen in this encounter, so many things could be felt racing through his mind, yet a center widening within, one of peace and belief in what was transpiring.

I saw the grip on the gun relax, his thumb reaching to the hammer to release it, then it fell gently into its cradle, the choice had been made. Sarah came over and stopped at my side on the second step. He walked over to his mother, put his hand on her shoulder. "Go home," he said. She began to protest to him but he leaned into her face. "GO HOME, NOW!"

Everyone began to break at the order. The protesters walked away and those that had come to aid Sarah began to return to previous actions before the psychic call. I wondered if they were aware of their diversion's purpose, or just followed some intuitive call to wander until they reached the old church.

The others from the center returned into its doors, while a

woman Sarah's age came down the steps to talk to her. Sarah introduced me, her name was Amanda. She was taller than Sarah, but so was everyone. A "valley girl" look about her, long straight blonde hair, dark tan (fake and bake) with huge almond sea blue eyes, yet her energy was radiating sincerity and calm, one I suspect was her usual demeanor.

Sarah did the introductions. "Amanda, Peter. Peter, Amanda." We shook hands, chance to do a quick energy scan amongst us spiritual types. Actually the custom of shaking hands originated for that purpose, when it was the only form of background check available.

"Well, Sarah, that was exciting," Amanda said. "What's for lunch, shootout at the OK corral?"

I like this woman, I thought.

We were talking and looking at the only remaining member of the protest, the gunman. He just stood there staring into nothingness. I sensed he did not know where to go or what to do. Where anger had been in me, now sadness took over about the man. Sarah left the step walking in his direction.

"I am waiting for you to call the police," he said at her approach.

"I am not going to call them, and I suggest you put that gun away before some passer-by does," she said to him gently.

"I was not going to shoot anyone, please believe that."

"I do believe that. I knew it when I put the gun up to my heart. I am evolved, not stupid. I trust what I sense in people, and your heart is not one of a killer. Just go home now and search your heart for what you believe, just you. Not your mother, your church or your education, just you. Then do what you need to become that, not what everyone else desires."

"I will, thank you."

With that he turned and left, we watched him walk down the alley into his future. As he walked I saw him dismantling the gun into its pieces, depositing them into separate dumpsters as he walked. One less gun in the world, human and metal ones. I would love to be a fly on the wall when he returns home.

Sarah returned to Amanda and I. She looked no worse for the wear, but seemed to be in deep analytical thought of these events.

"Well, that was interesting," Sarah said almost remotely.

Amanda put her arm around her shoulder and hugged her close. "C'mon, let's go in and have some coffee." She gently guided her towards the big doors. I followed them quietly, letting the event settle into my own consciousness.

The outside of the building was deceiving of its internal size, it was stepping into another world. It was like stepping into a time warp of religious domination the world once knew and respected, a museum of days long gone in the waves of modern understandings pushing antiquated beliefs into history. Yet one had to respect the work and design of it, the enormous undertaking of such a task. In many ways it was a monument to human ability and determination rather than the God it was to house.

All the pews had been removed, making the main room enormous, almost ominous. Looking to the ceiling made my neck stretch to the point of cracking, scanning the huge arched beams holding it in place for future generations.

Sarah and Amanda had stopped to accommodate my awe and curiosity, leaving me to my thoughts a few feet away. They whispered a little and Amanda walked off and disappeared into a side door.

Sarah stood beside me and touched my shoulder.

"Amazing, isn't it?"

"Yes, quite. These places were designed to set a mood of amazement and awe, to make one feel very small when entering, humility by design."

"Very much so. We removed the pews and sold them off through a local antique dealer to fund the place when we opened. We got a lot more than we were anticipating, so we got off to a good start. We rent this huge room out for yoga classes, aerobics, that sort of thing. It's also used for larger meetings and gatherings and for anyone that wants to teach classes. The acoustics are so good you don't even need audio equipment. It's booked most of the time, so we are happy for that."

"Very impressive. It's a very practical use for a very impractical building by today's standards. A lot of religions are selling these cathedrals off because of the cost to maintain them. You cannot run a place like this on contributions alone anymore."

"All too true. The core idea was to find ways to fund it, while being in service to the community as well. Finding the balance of input and output. Most spiritual centers are designed like a store, because they are, with classes being taught on the side, but the main premise is to sell the merchandise. Few, in my opinion, do the community much more good than any other store. We wanted something different."

"Imagine that, a spiritual center that serves the community in a practical way."

"Indeed, were still finding our center, so to speak. Being near a college I think is a plus, as our age bracket are more curious in trying new ideas and concepts, and this is a place that introduces them to alternative lifestyles and education. The building attached to this is administration offices and classrooms from the previous church occupancy, so we are able to utilize them as well. Some offices are used as classrooms, and we run a daycare center out of here as well. Being so close to campus, a lot of the staff there use it for their kids, and they are close enough to come by and see their kids."

"This is amazing, very purposeful and impressive in your design. I noticed a store sign on the side of the building before we were so radically distracted."

"Yes, the door leads to a bookstore and craft shop. It looks like a pretty typical spiritual store: books, crafts, incense and the usual items you would expect to find. Most of the crafts and artwork are bought locally from students and artists. A lot of the art is here on consignment. It's turning out to be a win-win for us and the local talent. Graduation has sold off a lot of the inventory we had."

"Well, you been a very busy little woman, haven't you?"

"Just trying to keep things real I guess. I always wanted a center, but was discouraged at the attitudes of most, a holistic storefront, but not much else of substance I felt when inside them. Classes by local teachers, most less qualified than the people they were teaching, a psychic reading office, that sort of thing. But serious teachers still had to forage for serious people desiring true education."

"Now who needs their cynicism bitch slapped away?"

"Yeah, yeah. But the desire grew in me when I was seeking help for myself, long before we met that morning. I resigned myself to the reality that I had to teach myself, so I did. Amanda and I learned together. Her parents were very strict Christians, which is a form of abuse unto itself."

"Got any coffee in this place?"

"Of course, sorry, I am being a rude hostess."

I followed her through a maze of hallways and offices, all buzzing with human beings doing whatever it was they do here, but all busy. Finally we landed in a kitchen the size of my apartment, alive with busyness also. Sarah expertly maneuvered her way through the kitchen and returned to me with two coffees and a smile, waving her finger to follow her back into the labyrinth. It was short walk to her office, the command center of this endeavor of human change.

It was a warm room, large but still a sense of coziness, her energy permeated the room like an aroma sweet to the senses, yet required a developed sensitivity to be fully aware of. The computers in the room were as comfortable as her collection of antique books. The old and the new coming together in a reality that time is still a theory.

She sat back in an antique desk chair that would dwarf a linebacker from the college team. Yet she seemed to be comfortable in it. I sat on a couch across from her.

"Do you want to talk about that little drama show outside?" I asked her.

"Not much to say really, the center had been getting hate mail from locals, Christians mostly, fundamentalists. Protesters are a part of the daily routine of this place. Change scares people, especially the kind we are into now."

"This is the time of all their prophecies, doomsday, end of the world stuff. You took a real gamble out there. You're lucky he turned out to be just a misguided soul and not a dedicated fanatic."

"If he wanted me dead he would have just walked up to me and done it. He wanted to shoot his mother, not me, I saw it in his mind and we 'talked' about that when we were eye to eye. But to tell you the truth, there is more emotion like that around these changes than I ever thought there would be."

"The prophecies are being fulfilled, but not as they desire them to be. Christianity's greatest failure has been in the fulfillment of their own prophecy."

"Many would argue, and do argue, that they are coming to pass. The wars, diseases, earthquakes, flooding. It all seems to fit their scenarios. I do not believe this, but it is a compelling argument."

"It is always a compelling argument, Sarah. The key is to not engage it, as arguing and debating these matters amounts to mental masturbation, intellectual mind games. It makes for good drama and ticket sales at the box office. What is happening on the Earth and in her is going to happen regardless of the reasons we assign to them. We do not control the Earth, and therein lies our root fear, something so much more powerful than us, and with an apparent agenda of her own. Even with the new developments in human evolution, you still cannot stop her quaking and shifting. We know diseases are largely human error in cause and cure, cancer may be down, but it is because human awareness is up, not the 'war on cancer' by medical research."

"I agree, but the new is struggling to find a place in an old paradigm. Religious and spiritual movements in human consciousness have failed historically, with the previous beliefs willingly trying to kill off the new ideas and ideals, like this morning. There are far greater powers willing to stop this from flowing into life, much greater than fanatics. Terrorism is well funded in all countries, someone very high up is agreeing this change must not occur. That guy in the street today was nothing compared to what we really face in the way of resistance. The solution is to let the old do what it does, and focus on building new without concern to the old paradigms. What will work from the old will find its place, and what will not will fall to their own choices. We only deal with the current reality when it intrudes into ours, like this morning's episode outside."

"Good, you saved me from having to say that to you. At the graduation there were people that did not belong, and in the protest this morning. I am sure you noticed two people there that were not at all interested in the protest, but were there anyway, and at the graduation, you were being photographed on cell phones by people that were not there to see anyone graduate. They are not surprised by what they are seeing I suspect, but at the speed with which it is occurring and the rapid escalation of ability."

"I sensed them, and some of the people here caught them on their phones as well. We are much more organized than anyone realizes. But to be honest, they are a part of this we keep watch on, but not lose sleep over. I had to touch that man to see what I was truly dealing with. But as I said, if I was supposed to be dead, I would be. Everyone here can do what

I did in the coffee shop, and you saw the group at the ceremony. Nothing we have done is a real threat. In fact I doubt they really understand the deeper ramifications of this change. As you said, the speed is amazing to me sometimes as well. But, it is what it is and there is no turning back now."
"I am also certain you're aware that there are powers in the U.S. and other countries that have used psychics for many decades. They are good at what they do and are far more advanced than people realize they are at this stuff."
"Yes, of course, we feel them probing all the time. Like a laser trying to burn into our consciousness, and it will intensify now that the ceremony made a public announcement of intent. But as I said, I have been here for four years training others, teaching them, and they have been guided to teach others close to them. I would imagine the majority of this sleepy little Ohio college is aware at this level. Their psychics will be very busy, this was a well networked graduation, the same thing occurred in Canada, Holland, Israel, Brazil, Argentina, and Peru, and ten other U.S. states."
"At least those that are willing to embrace it all. Others will do it like meditation, as soon as they feel better a little, they will stop, and when things get bad again, they will say meditation did not work. Our government is hardly the only one using these techniques and trying to develop them. But your networking will keep them overwhelmed for a little while, but do not underestimate their adaptability."
"I disagree, I agree it takes an embracing of it, but once you activate this, there is no going back to the way you were. In the past these practices relied on belief causing changes in consciousness, and it took prolonged practice to initiate changes at the biological levels, the micro levels. It set the stages for this time, preparing us for it, but history shows us. It was accomplished in only a few, those with strong minds and powerful beliefs, even the early monasteries could accomplish only a portion of their students to fruition. In the

new paradigm the speed we are evolving and enhancing ourselves requires a purging of negative beliefs that limit growth, using the practices for domination sets them back too far to recover in time."

"I am old school, I learned in the dusty basements of libraries in books I had to call days ahead for them to locate. It was an intellectual 'Indiana Jones' quest for the treasure of life. I started in Christianity and came full circle to quantum physics and microbiology. Touching all the others in between. Thank God the Internet was birthed, it was so welcomed by us all that seek. But during my searching, my biologies were changing also, the seeker becomes the sought, the treasure lies within the searcher, and it is not that I did not see it there. It just had to evolve itself within before I knew it. Alchemy in its purest understanding. Had this not occurred, I would have just seen an old man have a heart attack in that coffee shop, and you would have left without notice."

"This time is so profound, not because life is going to end, but because the changes will make all that was before this ancient history in its own time. Every biology on the planet right now is evolved to this in design, and all will awaken to full enlightenment, either by choice or circumstance, or die off as all genetic lines have that could not adapt, but in this time, it is the individual that is deciding if it will live on, not a genetic choice made within the entire line as in the past."

"Jesus is the prototype, not the exception. Control required separation of Jesus, God, and all considered divine from the human element. Now separation is not possible if the individual chooses to re-engage, making control not possible."

"Exactly."

"Indeed."

Sarah stood up energetically, almost bouncing on the floor. "Come on, I want to show you the daycare center and the other projects." She grabbed my hand not awaiting an answer, we were off again.

We shot down a long hall emerging in a wing with several large second story rooms. I could hear children at play from outside, like any playground in America this time of the day, kids are kids in any country. We then walked into a large room where a teacher was talking to a group of children around six to eight years old, all sitting on a carpeted floor. The teacher was reading a book to them, one written by the teacher, she was a student at the university also. The book was titled *Anything I Want to Be*.

"Is this place accredited?"

"No, and I am sure your next question is why aren't they in regular school right now. Those kids are discipline problems from local schools, usually we have twice that many. They come here for a few hours a day to relieve their regular teachers from their disruption, and we teach them self-learning skills and ways to build their confidence. They are taught a walking method of meditation, and weather permitting we have them outside in the woods and park as much as possible. I tutored privately when I first got here for money, and by working with some of the families, I was able to help with discipline problems as well, it just kind of spilled over to here after we opened."

"I see, I am also beginning to sense what this place really is."

"I knew you would, I was so excited when you said you were coming. There is so much to show you and to discuss. We're going to be each other's shadows for the next couple of days. I am going to introduce you to Ron, he is the director of the children's programs we offer and involve ourselves in."

We entered another office with a young man standing there. Very involved in thought, he barely noticed us walk in. I recognized him this morning and onstage at the graduation ceremony. Irish-looking man, red hair very shortly cropped, and a very round man too.

"Hi, I am Ron," he said with a genuine smile shaking my hand," Sarah said you were coming to visit, knew her back in the day she told us."

"Something like that I guess. Nice to meet you."

"Tell him what you're up to these days with the kids Ron," Sarah said.

"Well, basically we're an approved daycare center for kids from infants through middle school age kids. Most are in public school during the day, and the others are what we call drifters. Junior high and high school kids come in after school until their parents get home, or pick them up from here. A lot of them serve as aides and tutors to the young ones. We found it worked well on its own making the kids all aware of one another in the community, where they otherwise wouldn't even know any of them even existed. It's an alternative to latchkey programs. Kids helping kids.

"Parents that drop their kids here are aware we are a spiritual center with ideals based in human growth and enhancement, each is given a packet explaining how we handle things like discipline and health, food and also that we teach the kids self-energy skills and management. Of course these courses are available to the adults through the center also. Actually once the kids begin to learn it, the adults want to know about it."

Sarah chimed in, "We teach them energy principles as a nutrition course alongside food, explaining why they eat foods and what energies each food is providing them with, and what it will do for and to their bodies and mind as a result. It sounds very scientific for kids, but they grasp it with ease and complete understanding. They know from experience what a carrot versus a Twinkie will do to them mood wise. They are taught to use meditation skills to alter the effects on sugar when they have eaten too much. We use color charts as visuals of what energy and foods makes you feel good and which make you feel angry and crabby. They love it."

Ron continued, "We are concerned here with providing information that will aid kids through this transition in history. Sarah teaches them the transference technique you saw us doing at the ceremony yesterday onstage. They are easier to teach than the adults are because they are already 'wired' for it, before environmental influences overtake their openness. The idea of the entire layout for kids here, regardless of age, is to teach them they can learn anything they desire to, and what their design can allow them to become, regardless of the environment they are growing up in."

"It sounds like a lot for kids to learn, but I know you're correct. Anyone that thrived in abusive situations are living testimony to the reality of growth by self-will. I always imagined what we could do with kids that were taught their perfection as children. The kids in school that are honored are not the 'cream of the crop' just those that learned the game. The ones that change the human race are never noticed, or considered discipline problems, they are the wild genes of true change in the human gene pool."

"Precisely!" Sarah agreed.

"Yes, but here we deal with the ones that the other schools don't want to, because they are the ones we are looking for. The ones that need an alternative more than any. This center and others being opened around the world are geared to the kids in the countries they are in. The adult population and the elders have made their choices, but the kids just need to know how vast their choices are and how greatly they are designed, for greatness." Ron's passion for this was uncontainable in his dialogue, it is easy to see why Sarah turned this over to him.

"I agree, Ron. I cannot tell how much I agree. I have been watching those kids exercising across the hall while we've been talking. I see very definite yoga and tai chi in the movements. Those kids are what, three to six years old? That is absolutely beautiful, incredible."

"It's a beautiful thing," Sarah said. "The young man teaching it is a senior at the high school. A year ago he was looking at jail time for continuous drunk driving and just general trouble making."

"It all sounds a little la-la land to be true though. I believe what I am seeing, because there is no conflict in what I am sensing, but still. I wonder how the old regime out there will deal with this when it is attempting to usurp the status quo of life. I see things like lawyers screaming brainwashing, or a return to the good old days of witch hunting."

Ron responded first. "I see it too, and this morning's drama outside will increase as pressure on the old increases and the new moves into place, but we feel by educating the young to themselves and most importantly allowing them to be themselves, it will work easily by preference. What works is what people usually decide on. Seeing the kids after time here, they see it working and the kids want it to work."

"Within this is a discipline we borrowed from the ancient schools," Sarah explained, "from the Egyptian schools of Hathor, Tibet, and Mayan schools. Also employing the Hebrew of Qumran. Violations of rules means you're out. But we found they wanted back, and that decision is left to a body of students overseen by Amanda. They have to earn their way back in by independent study and demonstration of how they apply what they researched and studied. How will it enhance their life and others?"

"We have a ninety per cent return rate, and the process can be hard on them if they do not work to their potential. They know they are a part of something important to them here, and they want to be a part of it. To be honest here, it really doesn't take a lot of supervision in the daycare, because there is always a bunch of kids here wanting to help the little ones, even the infants. The high school kids can't wait to be with the little babies, it is a great learning experience for them, even the guys are always in there."

Sarah got a very serious look on her face as she began to speak. "Peter, you know the world of abused kids, molested ones, and ones that just live in shitty situations. We lose more than develop the determination to survive, you know not all kids are accidentally hit by cars, fall out of trees, or die from freak accidents. Here we teach them they have abilities they can use by design to know ahead of time what is waiting around the corner, who they need to run from before they are picked up, and when and how to purge emotions that will make them sick in heart and mind. We teach them here to use the abilities they were created with regardless of social acceptance of them. They learn from us, and mostly from one another they can be whatever they imagine they can be, just like the world is finally learning too."

"Well, that having been said, I need to make some calls and get back to work. Great meeting you, Peter, talk to you later, Sarah."

We said our goodbyes and walked around the kids' wing awhile. Sarah loved spending time here. No matter how you feel, being around kids can change your mood in a second. You had to really see what you were looking at to realize what was happening here. The way these kids were really developing, because at first glance, just kids, running and playing, arguing and being selfish. Just kids, being kids.

Sarah was speaking as we walked. "Ron has done some amazing things with the kids. He developed a musical form of meditation for the little ones to sing. Mantras are all about tone, so musical notes were the natural course for them to work with. Songs were created using specific notes and arrangement of them to create a mantra. They sing them every morning and before they go home, but you can hear them humming them outside too. They make them feel good, so they keep them in their minds."

"Where are we headed now?"

"To a basement level beneath the main church, Amanda's pet project and the heart of this place. I will be leaving you there for a while. I have a meeting with some people from Holland and Peru about opening centers similar to this in their towns. We'll meet up again for lunch."

V
Finding America

Sarah guided me down a stairway underneath the main room of the old cathedral above.

We landed at the bottom in front of two large metal doors. The whole area had a "service" look and feel about it, as if you wanted to pass quickly through it to get where you needed to go. But as I stood in front of the doors, my senses were at full alert, I could feel enormous activity behind these doors, far-reaching activity.

"This is Amanda's project, as I said. When she was four, her two-year-old brother disappeared from a mall, they never found him. It is why her parents went so far south into fundamentalist Christianity and became so self-absorbed, leaving Amanda to pretty much raise herself. She watched her parents pray constantly without results, until they just finally disappeared into the hopelessness of hoping."

"I sensed a deep sadness in her when I shook her hand. She is very powerful though, like you, like everyone I have met so far."

"Yes, like yourself too, Peter. I need to get to my meeting. Come on, Amanda is expecting you and looking forward to it, she loves showing off her work." She pushed open the door, and the energy hit me like a wind coming around a corner.

It was an amazing sight, it looked like we had just entered the bowels of a secret government instillation. There were people milling about, many staring into laptops and others standing at a wall full of computers and large monitors. On the screens were maps and real-time images of locations by satellite technology. Other screens had kids' pictures on them.

It looked like an office at the Pentagon at full alert. I did not need an explanation, this was about missing kids, all about finding them. At some of the desks, people were talking with uniformed police, while men and women dressed formally stood next to young men and women in jeans and T-shirts, talking and pointing at maps. The low hum of computers and printer sounds permeated the room, but the energy of accomplishment and heart centered concern was the air that one breathed in when entering this zone. There was no sense of frustration or failure anywhere to be found. In an atmosphere of dramatic circumstance smiles and laughter resounded, it felt almost wrong somehow, but I could not help but want to smile too.

Amanda appeared from one of the side rooms, spotted us at the door, and hurried over.

"Peter, good to see you again." She kissed Sarah on the cheek and turned to me. "So, I hear your ass belongs to me for a while."

"That's the plan I hear."

"Don't worry, I'll be gentle. I want to show you around this place. So much going on and we have a lot to talk about. Regardless if you know it or not, you put a lot of input into this project over the years you and Sarah have talked. Actually you put a lot of ideas into her head that you're touring today."

"I never knew."

"Well, you know now."

"I have always said, I do my best work when I don't know what the hell I am doing."

"We have all done good work. All of us here and around the world. We just need the U.S. to get on board. It's amazing how far behind the rest of the world we are in implementing new ideas into resolutions. But were making a lot of progress. Come and see."

Before we could take a step, the air was filled with a scream of joy, a young man was standing on his desk dancing like a quarterback that won the Super Bowl game in the last second of the game.

"YES! YES! YES! WE GOT HIM—WE FOUND HIM!"

The whole place erupted in applause, cheers and whistles. Everyone rushed to the desk he was standing on. Two men in suits pushed their way to his desk as the young man jumped down and pointed to a computer screen, on it was a satellite image of someone's back yard and a child about three on a swing.

"Enhance it!" one of the men said. He punched some keys on his keyboard and the image of the child zoomed forward and filled the screen.

"It's him! No doubt about it." He flipped out his cell phone and began talking to someone, giving them a state location and address. My senses told me that in a few moments police would be dispatched to that location and a child would be reunited with his family by dinner.

Smiles and cheers turned to tears and a sense of relief could be felt like a cool breeze on a scorching hot day, it just enveloped everyone in the room, even the tough looking guys in suits were rubbing their eyes, and looking for some Kleenex.

Amanda left my side and walked over to the young man and hugged him hard and long, then stepped back to look him in the eyes. "Good work, Mark, very good work."

The man that was on the phone, hung up and then shook Mark's hand and said, "Come on, let's get this kid home today." They focused back on the computer and started to work out the details together. Amanda came back over to me as others returned to their previous work, but the air remained electric, fully charged with excitement.

"Come on, let's get some coffee and chat awhile."

"You people drink a lot of coffee, but I am up for it."

"Some things remain constants in life I guess. I'll explain all this to you, but let's just get acquainted a bit first. We'll go in this room over here, it's a sort of a timeout room when things get stressful in here, and believe me they can."

It was a converted lunchroom I think, rather long and narrow, but painted in soft colors, light blues in a faux pattern, with the ceiling painted with a night sky effect. A couple of couches and lot of big pillows strewn about. We sat on a couch facing one another. I could feel Amanda deep scanning me with her eyes. So I spoke to her softly in a mind connection.

"Go where you like, I have nothing to hide."

"I know, I am very fast at this, and I wanted to know for myself if you were who Sarah believed you to be."

"Well. Am I?"

"Yes, you are, and that makes me very happy."

"I assume you have surmised our project's intentions out there?" she spoke openly.

"Pretty much, you locate missing children. It was hard to miss that excitement out there and its reason. Sarah told me of your brother just this morning. I am so very sorry for it and all you suffered as well. I am assuming it is why you're doing this."

"Correct on all points, Peter. I may never find Sam, my little brother, but the chances are far greater now with this place. I know it looks like any other place or organization might look doing the same work, high tech computers and satellite imagery software and the like. But we took our base operation from your suggestion to Sarah a few years ago to implement psychics in the search."

"I recall that talk with her. Putting them to work for things like missing kids and such. The government and police organizations have used them, but all the cynicism around them weakens them when they try to work with them. It is a futile effort in such negative surroundings."

"We agreed, here they are the heart of the program and the tech supports them, not the other way around. It was a 'hit or miss' thing in the beginning but once they realized they were respected highly for their ability, they took off with it. Even the workers and volunteers have increased their sensing abilities just working in this atmosphere. We have found over three hundred kids over the last two years, and even solved other crimes along the way."

"That would explain the police out there, I am assuming the suits are FBI people?"

"Yes, they are. They come here often, but still do so quietly and their offices in Cleveland and Columbus won't acknowledge any of it. In fact, Cleveland has most of us under investigation. We are what they classify as an 'Unknown Element' in their files."

"God, I love it. An 'Area 51' in little old Ohio. Who would have thought. This little operation has to cost a fortune, how is it funded?"

"Most missing children have a reward offered from family, and various organizations so we are given the reward when we find them. Sounds kind of mercenary I know, but the money would be paid regardless, and it all goes back into the same cause, so were at peace with it. Some of the equipment was donated by companies of people we have helped. It is a trust that what we need will come to us on the project, and the whole center, and it is working for us."

"Yes, trust, a biggy in a lot of people's lives right now. It seems so long ago that people trusted anything. But the illusions were pulled aside decades ago to reveal the truth of things in the world, seems like a slide down a shit mountain ever since."

"You're very tired, aren't you, Peter? I mean life tired."

"A little, yes I am. It has been a long road to here, and all this I am seeing today. Even the incident outside this morning is very saddening to me. That ignorance and superstitious religions can still change people into the opposite of their created designs, taking a human being and de-evolving them by belief into killers and assassins. That in our time preying on children is still so predominant in the human gene pool."

BEYOND THE MOMENT

"Sarah said you could be a tad melancholy. She says it is your age and the generations you have seen come before you and after into now. Jaded I think she called it. But we are doing great things in life now, and people are evolving into greatness like never in history. We are bringing more kids home alive now than when we started this. We are networked all across the country with other projects like this, some out of people's basements. Even into other countries, we are reaching out and becoming a race within a race."

"I know—I apologize for the generational gap in faith and promise."

"Not to worry, my friend. Sarah will make you a happiness junkie before you leave. No one escapes her energies. Believe me, even the guy with the gun will be coming here soon. You would be amazed at the history of a lot people here, even aghast at some."

"You really love her, don't you?"

"Don't you?"

"Yes, but not like you, you two have a true history and the way you two form one energy when you're in the same room, such profound lovers are hard to miss."

"I suppose you couldn't be fooled. Sarah was a bit concerned because of your age, people of your generation seem to tolerate it, but Sarah wanted your happiness too, for us. We have been in love all of our lives. When we were kids, we would sneak into each other's houses and sleep together, holding each other tight, we both only had each other. I would hold Sarah until the pain would pass from the old man's rape of her spirit, and she would talk to me until dawn about my parents and little brother. We have always been one energy and still managed to run and play as kids, fields and woods would find us there daily, climbing trees, just being kids. Miracles are not always profound ones, some are just arms around you when you feel life has no love except in fairy tales."

"It is a beautiful love story, Amanda, one I had seen and known in my imagery of her over the years as she opened up to me more and more. Like a daughter, I wish only her happiness, and I could not be more happy for this love you two share. It is love, and it is pure, forged in a child's love and need creating a powerful now and so much good for so many, what's not to love."

Amanda jolted into my arms and hugged me so tightly I thought I would stop breathing.

In my mind's heart I heard Sarah's voice. "Thank you, thank you, thank you so deeply."

"Right back at you, Sarah."

Amanda stood up and pulled me to my feet. "I have some other things to show you here, and I want you to meet the people that make this real."

"All right, just one thing before we go out there. I am very happy for you and Sarah. Love is not about sexes, it is about love, period. I think once we drop terms like gay and lesbian, we will see couples like you and Sarah as you truly are, pure, not fighting the straight people, but those that insist on making it a war, not about lovers and love. To tell you the truth, over the decades most same sex couples make me uncomfortable because they are about sex, or proving something, not about each other. Even the old lady this morning screaming Jesus at Sarah could not deny the genuine reality of the love you two feel. Enough said?"

"Yes, Peter, enough said."

"Okay, show me the miracles."

We went back into the room where people were still buried in their techno searching, crossed into another room almost as large, but with quite a different atmosphere. There was no one in it, but the energy was tremendous within its walls. As a room that had never been used for anything but meditation and prayer, the atmosphere would make the hardest of hearts become open and loving. I could feel and hear mantras resonating in the air.

The walls were covered in pictures, of children missing and recovered, some were flyers, others actual pictures of them sent from the families, as was the ceiling covered in pictures as well. I only had to look up once and gaze at them to feel they were the ones that had passed on, the ones recovered in death, those that would not be returning home, yet they had the gentlest energies of all the pictures in here. No lights were on when we entered, but once inside there was no need for them, as the ceiling radiated a glow I would need no explanation for.

"This is where our psychics work, where they group together in the midst of all these kids and sit until they can combine their power to seek them out. They have gotten so good at this, they seek by trying to contact the child directly. Sarah taught them the purging method and now they are more powerful than they could have been in this lifetime. The clothes and toys you see are actually belongings of the kids themselves, sent by their families to assist in contacting them, energy to energy sort of thing."

"Yes, I can feel the power of it all in here. So much to read in the energy, so many little voices I can hear. I could live in this room."

"Everyone says that. When the people out there get too overwhelmed they come in here, and when one of our babies are found dead, we all come in here and meditate and pray together. We contact the family in our own way to tell them. It sometimes allows the child to say goodbye to the family also, through our people, closure comes in a new way for us all."

I was about to respond to her, when a huge feeling of danger came over me, it was engulfing me like a cloud. I could feel myself being pushed into action from unseen hands on my back, words screaming in my mind, "GO—NOW! Move, man!"

I looked at Amanda, her eyes widened with almost panic in them. "What is it? WHAT?"

I grabbed her hand and pulled her like a rag doll behind me

in to the tech room. Words came out my mouth before I knew I was saying anything.

"GET DOWN—NOW—THERE'S GOING TO BE AN EXPLOSION, DOWN NOW, GO—GO!"

No one doubted it for a second, everyone began to fall to the floor and diving under desks.

I saw the FBI people going into their training modes, pushing people down onto the floor and covering them with whatever they could find, but not seeking cover for themselves.

I still held poor Amanda dragging behind me toward the door leading up the stairs. Halfway up the stairs she took the lead, knowing I did not know my way around.

"WHERE THE FUCK ARE WE GOING?"

"FRONT DOORS!" I screamed. "FRONT DOORS—HURRY SARAH IS HEADING FOR THEM."

Amanda's pace doubled at that revelation, screaming Sarah's name the whole way through the maze. I could hear the FBI's footsteps running about ten yards behind us, trying to stay with the maze too. I was following her voice now screaming out Sarah's name, she had long ago disappeared into the hallways.

I hit the door to the main room finally, where surreal time took over us all, it was happening so fast now, another dimension was reached in our senses. I felt myself hit the floor of the main room as I entered stepping into slow motion after leaving light speed. I saw Sarah about ten feet from the front door, Amanda was about halfway across the floor still screaming her name, and the three FBI people were closing in behind me.

I saw Sarah turn her head slowly to see Amanda's face and her expression turned to one of fear at seeing her, then it happened. Deafening sound filled the room like a dam breaking under the water's demand to be released. The huge oak doors exploded inward with pieces of stone from its mighty frame coming in at us in a full rage for having been torn from their ancient home. Sarah was flying through the air like a kite just let go of in a heavy wind. Amanda flew backwards with her face demanding a change of direction, falling to deaf ears of circumstance still reaching in the wind for Sarah. The whole building was shaking as if God's hand was rocking it with a furious anger for some unknown offense.

I flew back into the doorway of the hall I just emerged from taking down the three agents in my flight, hitting them like bowling pins on an alley of no concern. I was lying there, conscious, but unable to move, still hearing the rainstorm of stone and wood hitting the floor of the cathedral's heart room. I sensed the agents behind me trying to regain their faculties and balance, several attempts to stand were thwarted by the body's refusal to move yet. We were covered in dust and debris even behind the protection of the hallway's walls. I was scanning with my mind frantically but heard no replies. I struggled to my feet and stumbled into the main room. Sarah and Amanda were both lying motionless arms outstretched towards one another, but still a good ten feet apart. I made my way towards them praying with each step, demanding their aliveness in my mind directly into the vastness of the universe, I could feel my inner screaming voice filling any void between myself and God. Angels were being blown out of the way by my screams into the court of God. "Don't you dare take them home!"

I was leaning over Sarah when the agents joined me in seeking the girls' life signs. I barely heard them giving each other orders. One stayed with me while the other two headed back into the building to check the rest, and to make haste to the daycare area.

"They're alive!" I heard him say—then all went dark.

VI
Eyes in the Sky

When I came to, I realized it had only been a few moments. Sarah and Amanda were still in the same positions I had seen them before. The agent was standing just outside the hole left in the front of the building. He was looking intently at everything, gathering evidence I presumed. I went to stand up and realized the effort had sent me to the ceiling of the great room, and (minor detail here) my body was still lying on the floor unconscious.

"Well this is just fucking great!" I thought.

I was aware of everything, I could hear sirens screaming in the near distance from more than one direction, the FBI agent was now on the phone, and one that had been in the blast area was returning up the hallway I had come from. She was walking fast, but I did not detect an urgency in her that would reveal more people hurt, everything else "felt" good except the immediate blast site—here. Although in a few moments we were going to be engulfed in the chaos of EMS, police, and rescue workers. I could already see people crowding the front of the church to get a look, I also saw the man from this morning across the street, looking very bereaved and crying. The room was covered in dust, stones broken away and blood, even what appeared to be body parts near the front entrance. A suicide bomber? Here in Ohio?

Okay, first things first here—am I dead?

"No, you're not, thank God," it was Sarah's voice. "Nor is Amanda or myself, thank God again."

"Well, we all sure look dead down there."

"Well we're not, if we were there would be a whole different approach to this conversation. Now look over here, above where the doors were. See the two shiny orbs?"

"Yes, I do."

"Well, that's us!" It was Amanda.

"But we're not dead, we're free floating orbs of consciousness, but we're not dead?"

"Jesus, let it go, we're NOT dead," Amanda yelled.

"OK, OK. So what are we doing up here? Orbs can yell? How cool is that!"

"We suffered some damage that is going to take a few days of being unconscious to heal for all of us. Our bodies need deep sleep right now. The agent is waiting out there for the rescue people, but we need to get into the hands of our own people before they arrive. I am sending out a psychic message. We have a healing center here, but we need to get some place safer for now, this isn't over yet I feel," Sarah said.

"Our people know to get us to safety in an emergency, safety meaning in the hands of our own," Amanda chimed in. "Ron went to the daycare at the first signs of trouble. The kids were outside, and the babies were moved out as well. They are all over at the elementary school now. Everyone else is fine. The blast stayed in this area, no damage anywhere else except superficial."

Sarah moved closer to the hole to see outside. "Wait for it," she said softly.

"GUN!" we heard someone yell outside from the crowd. There was instant pandemonium in the crowd, people were running, yelling, and screaming, the agents flew down the steps into it all trying to find the source.

In the same instant, people began pouring into the great room from three separate entrances, two ran immediately to the front and watched, signaling the others.

"Go, go," they whispered gruffly with hand gestures. A swarm of people came in and broke into three teams: one team heading for each of us. Two women over each one of us were scanning us with their hands, while the other did a hands-on scan. They all stood up simultaneously and one woman snapped her fingers as an OK to move us. We were placed onto hand stretchers and whisked into the same doors they had appeared from. The two at the doorways used soft brooms as they backed their way out leaving not a single footprint behind. In what seemed like seconds, everything looked the same, except the three bodies on the floor were gone.

The "GUN" cry was a diversion to empty the room and distract anyone from inside while this precision operation took place, it was an amazing sight to see. They probably could have done it right under the agents' noses.

"I do love that woman. She does amazing things with a naturalness that can be scary at times. That little display of slight of hand was done by Theresa, she organizes all the events here and outside. She also takes good care of our exposure out there, believe me, she has been prepared for this for some time."

"Does she know who did this?" I asked.

"Probably, but if she doesn't now, she will soon. Nothing escapes her," Amanda replied.

"I know when I started this with Amanda, she was the quickest to understand where we were heading and how to get there. She was always very clear on how to navigate through the transition period we're now into. She has been a holistic teacher for decades and she has expertise in many areas. She has trained all the healers here herself, and forced them beyond healing modalities into energy alignment for pure enhancement. Her people are masters at opening DNA to its full twenty-two strand potential."

"You were to meet with her next after me, Peter. She has been anxious to meet with you, and to pick your brain."

"She almost got the chance to pick it up, off the floor."

"Believe me, she will not rest until she knows every detail, and how she missed it coming.

She was out of town visiting her daughter, I did not even know she had returned until I saw her swooping out onto the floor to gather us up," Sarah said.

"The agents are going to freak when they come back in and see we are not there," I said.

"It's not really a concern I have right now. Theresa will handle it, and well. She and Ron work closely together, the kids are their priority, they are the future in a more profound way than anyone on this planet realizes. They are protected like God seeds, because they are. As individuals, they will be told the truth, since we work together with them in the child abductions, Theresa will work with them to come up with something the Bureau will accept to cover their professional asses. But no one except Theresa and Ron will know where we are, and knowing her, we'll be moved a few times before she is satisfied we are safe."

"That is some intense loyalty from people."

"Yes it is, because it is a loyalty to self, all selves. The dichotomy is resolved in this new paradigm. We are all becoming powerful, powerful individuals through this, yet there is a sort of 'one mind' we all share consciously, yet silently," Sarah explained.

"So does this conversation get shared in this new united collective consciousness?"

"Yes and no. It can be if someone connected would choose to tap, but most just walk the walk every day, as our consciousness is directed to keep it moving forward. It is hard to explain, but I think you get the idea. For instance, Theresa is tapped into this, because she is aware of our concern with our bodies, and she has a concern with our consciousness, so the common concern keeps us connected. She is not listening per se but is aware."

"I get it, as I am aware we are communicating, but am also aware that you and Amanda are carrying on another 'talk' even as we do, a very personal one, and we're all staying very aware of what is going on down on the ground. Multidimensional awareness as one awareness, the key is the expansion to process it all as one dimension. Ta DA!"

"Exactly," said Amanda.

At that point the orbs seemed to become one orb of energy, and we found ourselves far and away from the activities of the cathedral. We just seemed to appear in an unknown dimension of luminous solidity of energy. I could see Sarah and Amanda as form, much like those Christmas tree glass ornaments, seeing it and through it simultaneously, depending on how you played with your focusing ability.

Sarah and Amanda were standing side by side on seemingly nothing at all, but as they moved, I could see energy supporting them like the crest of a wave, they were walking towards me, and appeared to be walking on water, but the splash around their feet was light, not water, as it calmed it was totally invisible again. I felt quite natural and comfortable here. I somehow knew this place of consciousness.

"I know where we are," I said. "I wrote about this place long ago. I called it the 'Sea of Glass' when writing about where I went when I left my body during abuse. This is where we all know each other from, isn't it?"

"Yes, and no. But it doesn't really matter in the present. Hanging on to time dimension just makes you frustrated in these dimensions, or any for that matter. I suggest we just enjoy the calmness of it." Sarah was speaking.

"We have a lot to figure out while our bodies recover. We must plot a course through this period of transition in real time. Human life is what matters and we must find a way around the violence coming from the fear, a way to neutralize it before it occurs, like today's explosion," Amanda thought to us all.

I walked, floated, whatever over to them. "I know how this place works I think." I waved my hand across the floor of us and thought of the cathedral at the same time. The floor began to shimmer and a window appeared with the imagery of what was occurring there.

We could see the police and FBI agents walking and talking, firemen milling about, while other investigators were collecting evidence. Forensic people were bagging body parts, it was a human bomb after all. A tall woman was talking to the FBI people from the child recovery program.

"Is that Theresa?" I asked.

"Yes it is," said Amanda. "She is working her magic with the FBI, I am sure explaining what happened to us. The agents familiar with us know we are a very self-contained group and will not be surprised at the actions taken, but they will be deeply concerned about the attention this will draw to the Bureau in Cleveland. Until now we were just a spiritual fringe group not worth focusing much on. Now they will certainly be taking a more serious look."

"Theresa is a tall drink of water, around six feet it appears, very intimidating appearance in that long dress and hair down to her legs. Around fifty?"

"Yes, somewhere around that I think. She walks with a sense of confidence to be sure. She has been very helpful with the young women in raising their self-esteem, and the men respect her without even being sure why, they just sense her mystique holds a lot knowledge. Amanda and I have learned a lot from her. She is a professor at the college in quantum physics and instructor at the center, amongst other things."

"I think we were bombed by the old woman, I saw her son outside in the crowd that gathered. I am sure some of the larger body parts are hers, from the hair fragments I am seeing there on the floor just inside the door, and the clothing pieces, same material as her dress."

"You're right," Sarah said, "but there's something that feels wrong about her being the trigger for this. Can you sense deeper, Peter?"

"The son is not a part really. I sense him to be too confused to make a clear choice like this one would require, too torn between his own beliefs and sense of loyalty to mom. He stays with the church because he fears being wrong more than anything, a real fire and brimstone upbringing. Mom is—was a fanatic and they are easily manipulated with the right dialogue of Jesus needing soldiers for fighting Satan, like the Middle East today. Add religion to poverty and fear, you have a cloaking device for political agenda to hide a visible and unnoticed army of dangerous soldiers, the kind that will gladly blow themselves up for God. She was a pawn to someone—whom?"

"I agree with that sense completely," Sarah said and Amanda nodded in agreement.

"This is smaller version of what is happening with Islamic terrorism, and America as the devil. Islam senses great changes on her horizon, and their unconscious sensitivity tells them whatever it may be is coming from America, but being unable to pinpoint it, destroying the home of change is the only possible resolution to the dilemma. Jihad and holy wars are never a part of religion or its prophecies, they are added later as an option for the religions survival, or so they think. Christianity however took a different approach when they realized war wasn't working for them, they removed the main part of the evolutionary equation, they separated God, Jesus, and their attributes from the human growth possibility. Someone is aware that the center is a source of change, an indefinable change, yet with the powers they do not understand, the most threatening is an apparent ability to live outside the box, their box."

"I and Sarah surmised a long time ago that if we wanted to free of our pasts, we had to not succumb to traditional approaches of healing, but create something entirely new, to recreate ourselves in actuality, not metaphorically. We studied all the old traditions as you did also, but as you also surmised, they were designed to take us to this place in time and from here, it was up to us."

"As in our conversations, Peter, over the years, we also began to look at the practices being able to evolve also. Meditation, authentic yoga, even the art of prayer having an evolution of their own. Seeing this led us to the sciences as it did you. We began to see ourselves as sum totals, as you say all the time, not pieces trying to integrate with spiritual practices. We are complete, and any idea or ideal that causes us to separate ourselves in any form is a false understanding. Once we let this sink in things began to change in quantum leaps, as in the coffee shop that morning. I did not initiate that, I allowed it. I saw him, we locked eyes and the rest occurred as a natural process. As in Zen, it is done when we do not know it is Zen, it just is the way we do things without conscious thought."

"The more Zen was written about, the farther it walked from its truth," I said.

Sarah continued, "What happened on the stage at graduation was a simple allowing, each allowed their true feelings to emerge, and it was only when they left them did true feeling find its true source.

When the old man locked eyes with me, what was his left me, and returned to its source.

Lovers do this when they fight, overload causes the process to unfold, the emotional bag breaks. That morning I allowed it to happen without the anger as a catalyst for the feelings to flow. My Charka's aligned and configured it all in a new way, because I am enlightened, meaning I have twenty-two strands of DNA sending and receiving coding, aligning higher vibrations to carry them."

"Sarah and I worked at unity, being one, only, even as children we talked of these things, because abuse is a great awakener of abilities some spend lifetimes acquiring. For a long time we were stuck it seemed, something was holding us back, then you found it, the idea we were a series of many past lives, another diversion from reality. You said you saw yourself as a continuum, one single life, composed of many experiences, yet just one life through the time space continuum. Once we meditated on this, all fell into place."

"I recall that talk we had, it was revealing to me also. Many experiences within our biologies, the body total houses the total mind. We carry in them every experience ever felt while interacting with the us in that continuum, both male and female. Once the continuum is realized and embraced, even the sex differences disappear, one body, one mind, one. Spirit is realized to be a verb, not a noun, defining the motion between micro and macro."

Just then Amanda waved her arm across the ceiling of our energy room and the universe appeared above us. "I so wanted to do that since we got here."

We just stood there, energy to energy in complete loving reality that in oneness we are as infinite as the universe we were gazing into, we were but atoms in this vastness, but felt as close to it as a lover in the act of making love, in all its vastness it knew us intimately and loved us the same.

VII
Pivotal Moments

Theresa stood in the great hole that was once the entrance to the cathedral. She scanned the scene deeply with evolved senses, and searched for the FBI agents. It had been only an hour since the explosion, she turned and looked at the room, feeling tears demanding release, but pushed them back. "Not now, later," she thought to herself.

The agents had realized the gun cry was a diversion, or someone's sick sense of humor, but abandoned the pursuit nevertheless. She had asked two of the young men to seek the agents out and bring them to her as quickly as possible. The gun diversion had sent most of the curiosity seekers home, the area had been roped off and things were pretty calm compared to the last hour.

Theresa stood there in the middle of the doorway, looking more ominous than the cathedral itself. Her seasoned face was still projecting a timeless youth, even for a woman in her fifties, her very long straight black hair cascaded down to her waist like a waterfall of elegance, framing her face with a mystique that made her green eyes seem an endless road into the woman. Her habit of wearing long flowing dresses gave her a look that made the mind confused as to what time dimension she was standing in, a look as if from a religious order that was not yet a part of the human arena.

A young man came up the stairs towards her, she leaned to hear his whisper. The agents were on their way to her office in the center, reluctantly leaving the position they felt was their trained duty to protect. She then returned some unheard instructions to the young man's ear and gently kissed him on the crown of his head and he scurried off.

She turned and lifted the hem of her dress so as not get it

dirty from the dust and debris, and appeared to float across the great room and disappear into a long hallway leading to her office.

When she arrived, the three agents were there, it was a large room, devoid of any personal touches, just an office that stated, "this is a place of focus on intent." There were three chairs already there for the people, and one large antique chair one would expect to find in a high end office of wealth and power, with a small table next to it. One of the men and the woman were sitting, and the other man was pacing when she swept into the room. She had a sense of presence that dwarfed the others immediately, seeming to strip them of all their roles and illusions of themselves, ensuring that the conversation would be human being conversing to same.

"Quite a morning, Theresa," the pacing agent stopped to say.

"Indeed it is," she replied, adjusting her dress in her seat.

"Where the hell are they, Theresa?" he asked in a demanding tone.

The other two began to squirm in their chairs, anticipating a very heated argument brewing. These three had been working with the child find project for a couple of years now, unbeknownst to the official Bureau headquarters, so they were well aware of Theresa's abilities and rigidity to being manipulated in any way. This could get ugly, they were all thinking.

"I thought the EMS had transported them to the hospital. I call there, and guess what?"

"They weren't there?" she said with almost a smile.

"Don't fuck with me on this, Theresa!"

"I assure you, David, I would never 'fuck' with you on this matter, or any other for that matter."

"I'm sorry, really, this has just hit close to home. We all like those girls, and who the hell is this new guy that just arrived? How can you be sure he didn't bring this with him? He seems kind of shady to me. I saw him at the graduation ceremony."

"He is friend of Sarah's, enough said on him for now. Let's get to it, shall we? Here is what is going to happen next, my friends. First of all, does the Bureau know you are here, and of this event?"

"No, they think what they always have when we are here. We're out in the field doing investigative work, looking for the kids. I haven't called this in yet because I can't tell them anything except there has been an explosion of unknown origin. But the local police have been all over it, and there were some reporters out there. We didn't find anything on the gun either, so there isn't much to report."

"Good, please sit down, David, you need to relax." There was deep compassion in her voice.

"Where are they, Theresa? Please tell us, we do care, you know about them."

"I know you all do. Please listen to me carefully. This is going to be a pivotal point in all your lives, right here, now, in this room. Your lives will be very different when you leave here. Sarah, Amanda, and Peter are in our care, they are fine and being very well cared for, more so than the hospital could provide for them. We have our doctors and healthcare people that work with us, and until I am sure it is safe and this incident is a singular event, they will remain where they are."

"You cannot do that, they are an integral part of a serious crime."

"I have done it, and it will remain so. Listen to me, please let me finish. I assure you they are going to be quite fine. This evening's paper is going to report on the explosion, and it will say that it was of unknown origin, probably a gas leak under the main doors, but is being investigated further, but the gas leak will be the inevitable finding."

"And how the hell do you know it is going to say that? There is something else too, Theresa, the small matter of the splattered body parts all over the steps! Jesus, think about this will you please!"

"I assure you, I have thought about it. I know the paper will say that, because I wrote it, as will the TV news, because I wrote that script too. As for the unfortunate woman that was caught in the blast, her son is downstairs talking with some of our people now. I also assure you he will not present any problems at all, he was a part of an earlier incident that took the wind out of any sails he may have tried to launch."

"You're a scary woman sometimes, you know that, Theresa?"

"I have heard that rumor. You keep interrupting me, don't be rude, David. I know this is not a simple matter of a gas leak, the escalation of threats has been gradual but steady lately.

"After the graduation ceremony we anticipated something, but I must admit, not to this scale so soon, but that is the story going out and it will be the final word on the matter, and frankly, there isn't anything you can do or say to alter its reality. Look, all three of you.

"Here is your reality, you have all been rapidly promoted over the last two years as a result of your accomplishments in locating so many lost children, dead and alive, you're local heroes in the Cleveland office, and very well paid, and all of us sitting here know why that is. They leave you alone and don't hold you accountable for much because of your records. If they knew where you were most of the time and now, it would be quite a different story, would it not?"

"That feels a lot like blackmail," Angie, the female, said.

"Mamma always said 'if it looks like a duck, waddles and quacks like one, it's a duck' and this is a duck, Angie," Theresa said staring, deeply into her eyes.

Theresa continued, "Our association over the last few years has been a win-win for everyone, especially those children lost out there, there is no reason this has to alter that, and won't as far as we are concerned. But, I think you're beginning to realize how organized and interconnected this center is to the community, the state and to the entire country, even globally. Within a week this building will look as it did before the blast. As we speak, there are contractors heading here for the foundational damages and other damage throughout the building, permits are waiting for the ink to dry. There are freemasons from Amsterdam on a plane this very moment, and there are two dozen Amish buggies about an hour away with carpenters, stone workers, and women to help feed everyone, and comfort the children that were here at the blast time. The other children will be in the classrooms tomorrow morning as usual."

"It is still a crime scene," said Angie.

"No, it is not. It is the scene of an unfortunate accident, with an unfortunate victim blown into so many pieces no evidence of a bomb remained."

"You, you went in and removed all the fragments, didn't you?" Angie accused.

"Indeed."

"Don't you want to know who did this and why?" David inquired.

"We will, David, and we will keep you all in the loop, but this is our baggage, not yours. We know the woman was the bomb, but she was not the source, nor was her church. She was duped by someone else, used like all fanatics are. This was an accident, and this meeting is closed to this subject until I reopen it. Now I need you all to consider your futures in this center's operation, you now have a glimpse into us you did not before this. We are more than just a lonely outpost of psychics and spiritual people. Search your hearts over the next couple of days, and we will talk again. Karl, you have had not much to say," she said as she addressed the final agent.

"I know when to talk and when to listen, this was a listening time. You scare the hell out of me, Theresa, and so does this place, but change is scary, and this place is change on a scale the world has not ever seen. I am along for the ride, and those kids are what I am all about, as long as we keep finding them, I am happy to leave you to your business, because I know too that there is no stopping whatever the hell you are up to."

"Indeed—I suggest you all get some needed rest, then if you would help them get the child find area up and running we would really appreciate the help there. Then please join us all for dinner. The Amish women are amazing cooks, a veritable feast of flavor, and they are delightful to spend time with. You helped them retrieve two of their kidnapped children a few years ago, they have been awaiting the chance to meet and thank you."

"I still think you're wrong, Theresa, but it is what it is for now," said David.

"Yes it is, David, for now," Theresa said, with a slightly detectable smile and a faraway look in her green eyes.

Theresa sat quietly for a time after everyone had left, simple reflection is often the best in times of turmoil. Think, do not dwell, and never enter the realm of "what could have been" as there is often no escaping the thought streams.

She thought about her visit with her daughter and two grandchildren in Washington State. She visited the center her daughter ran there and now wondered if such events would occur there. But she had sensed no such vibrations around it, as she had here, cutting her trip a day short to return.

She was feeling fatigue from the day's events, so she closed her eyes and realigned herself.

She felt her crown chakra vibrate and saw white light begin to pour into her body, flowing down through all her chakras, a warm glow was engulfing her spreading outward to the limits of her flesh, then beyond. Her breathing was aligned to the energy flowing in and out of her, and strength returned to her with each inhale. Her eyes opened without sight as darker energies flowed from them and dissipated into the room and disappeared.

Slowly life and light returned to her eyes and she stretched to loosen tensed muscles and felt renewed.

It amazed her how things that use to take hours to accomplish for renewal could now be done in moments, things that needed years to come to fruition could be accomplished in a few weeks.

VIII
Logistics of Spirit

Sarah waved her hand and the center appeared in a portal. She brought up the room with Theresa sitting alone after her talk with the agents, she was crying with her head in her hands. A stream of love went to her from Sarah's heart for the woman that had showed her so much kindness when she arrived there. Theresa had sat for hours listening to Amanda and herself, their plans and desires. She was the center's mother, the crone to everyone with heart, wisdom, and unending compassion for everyone.

Amanda and I had joined Sarah viewing the image, when another orb appeared near us, it was Theresa's voice within its essence. I looked at the portal to see Theresa in meditation, then back to the orb, now taking form. It was as watching water form into a being, with light along the edge lines keeping essence from free floating away, a beautiful sight to behold.

"Why were you crying?" Sarah asked gently.

"Been a rather stressful day, my dear, you're sleeping through it, remember?" Typical Theresa comment. "Tears of release and joy, everyone is alive there. Cause for celebration if you ask me."

"Yes, yes, cause for celebration, Theresa," Amanda piped in.

"Seriously, Theresa, how are you? You walked into a bit of a mess after returning from your daughter and grandbabies. That retrieval of us was amazing by the way."

"My daughter and her family are doing amazingly good, her center is growing rapidly. The grandchildren are growing at the same rate, fast and well, thank you, all is good there.

Retrieving all of you was necessary, it contained the damage from the public's drama, and finally got those agents into the loop of us. David and Karl are sincere in their work with us and finding the children, Angie is the mole. We must operate under the assumption she has been fully reporting back to the Bureau in Cleveland."

"We knew that, she is also a trained psychic, it's how she is sliding in under the radar of the others. Our intuitives warned us, remember?"

"Yes, I recall. So nothing new then, we just have validation. That's the beauty of all this, it cannot be deterred from its course. But a massive explosion can reroute the day's agenda to be certain. How did I miss it coming?"

"We all missed it," Sarah continued. "I was heading out to the university for my meeting when I heard Amanda screaming for me. Another minute and I would have walked right into it, hearing her slowed my pace considerably. Timing, timing, timing."

Theresa turned to me. "We owe you a debt of gratitude, Peter. Your sensing of danger saved her, we are very grateful."

"As am I."

"So, you're Sarah's friend. I was beginning to think you were her imaginary friend since even Amanda had not met you," Theresa said in a half laugh.

"No, I am as real as you," I said.

"Okay, let's get to business, shall we," Theresa continued. "I have lots to do as we speak. You are all doing fine, as I am sure you're sensing. There are healing doctors with you now, no broken bones or internal damage, just a lot of shaking up from the impact. Rest is the order of the day."

"Healing doctors, still sounds like an oxymoron," Amanda said.

"New times, new language," Sarah retorted.

"We'll be returning with you, Theresa," Sarah injected. "I feel we all agree we will be fine, and we're anxious to get back to things. What do we know?"

"We know it was the fanatic woman that blew up. She was

wired with just dynamite, no detonator. We found no pieces of any trigger whatsoever, we did find a bullet in the room, thrown from her body when she exploded, so we surmise she was shot to detonate her. Our intuitives feel she was going to pretend to be a bomb to get your attention and threaten you, they also feel strongly she was duped into the charade and it backfired on her. They questioned the son also, and he remains clueless, and we have no reason to feel otherwise. His grief was genuine as is his shock at her doing this. He remains torn between grief and relief. I consider him out of the equation."

"We agree with that. We must find a way to navigate this to a peaceful conclusion, Theresa. Loss of life is not acceptable, any life. The woman was following her beliefs just as we are, and fanatics are only fear filled, and fear is no reason to die. We cannot be brought into the drama, and that is what this is in its essence, an attempt to draw us back into the old paradigms of fear and its offsprings of hate and rage. 'Someone' feels if they attack we will have to fall into a defensive posture, fear. We must avoid the road backwards," Sarah counseled.

Amanda spoke gently. "Love is our power and it must prevail, will prevail. Not love as we once all knew it, but as a force stronger than any aggression we are facing. This is a plot to scatter the energy and make us stay in a mode of regrouping it, constant recentering of ourselves and the collective unity. We cannot even get trapped into seeking the conspiracies or the conspirators, any focus there takes our sight away from love."

"You're pretty wise for a young one. But then again age is an antiquated concept now too," I said.

"Oh, you can speak!" Theresa chided.

"You're going to try to bust my balls, aren't you?"

Sarah and Amanda broke into laughter that seemed to resound through the whole universe, as if the angels were laughing along with them. But it was the talk of love that brought us back to ourselves, where we needed to be and the realization we wanted to return to our bodies. From here we could clearly see the healing pace was also under our control, our ability to heal as rapidly as we desired to. We are aligned for it, evolved for it, and our bodies were one with our consciousness, so belief becomes undeniability of reality. No divisions. Everlasting life.

"In answer to your question, Peter, no. Besides I undressed you for the healers, looks like someone already did that."

"OUCH. That hurt. True, but still hurts. I like this woman!"

"We knew you would," Amanda said. "You both have the same sense of humor, we welcome the relief."

"Ah, good to know I serve some purpose in life. I agree that we cannot be swept into the drama. That is like walking into a vampire's house and bleeding for them. But they will not stop you know, they will be enraged when we emerge in the morning alive and well. But it strikes me that we have the tactical advantage here. No fear. Fear can be turned to form a defensive line, without us putting any of our energies into it. If love is water, fear is mud. Move the mud to allow the water to flow by the water's own force," I said.

"Interesting analogy, Peter, very," Theresa said. "Fear is a very dense energy, like mud, mud cannot stop the water's flow only slow it down and cause it to have to separate to flow forward. Bring the water together back into a wave, and it moves the mud back onto itself."

"Yes, actually forming the bank to route the water forward, the larger the wave, the more the water creates the landscape, eventually transforming the mud into a foundation for growth of new life. What appears to the eyes as destruction and chaos, but it is creating anew as it passes and changes everything," I pondered openly.

Sarah began to walk in a circle.

"Are you all right over there?" Amanda inquired of her.

"Yes I am, were onto something here, but were not there yet. We all feel it!"

Theresa began the breakdown. "The graduation was streaming, that went out into those the ten people onstage knew, sending out the toxins from themselves, then the love came along to neutralize the toxins, because these were people that loved each other, but within minutes it was waving into everyone, the energy formed its own wave, finding its own path. Like your water, Peter. Before becoming a wave it had to stream through the fear in the crowd, any new sensation felt, knee jerk responses as fear instinctively, but the love recreated the terrain of emotions being felt. The individual streams of love sought each other out, pushing the fear aside like mud, until it was the dominant energy there."

"Yes of course," Sarah cried out. "Quantum physics of like attracting like even within the negative. Purging negative emotion is the same natural principle. You cannot purge negativity by focusing on it, it only attracts more in the focus, but attracting the positive begins to fill the mass of self with same, pushing the negative out without any effort."

"It's why therapy doesn't work according to its own principles. The error is thinking that focusing on the negative experiences alone purges them, assuming positive will just flow in," Amanda added.

"PEOPLE, let's take a deep breath, shall we? Are we breathing here? We're getting off on a tangent here. This discussion could run for days. I suggest we get focused back on track. What is the track?" I said.

"I agree totally," said Theresa, "and the track is navigating to avoid being blown up! Something I think we are all in favor of. I know I am."

Sarah walked over to us and turned to face us. "We're going to her funeral, the woman that died. I have something to say to that congregation. I would like you three to be there, please. Now, as for navigating through this, as I see it, there is nothing to navigate through, only to observe while we continue to grow within the old paradigm. It is a great feeling to be near someone that loves Jesus enough to love themselves as reverently and sacredly, with equal emotion. To be near love that silences someone as to not miss one sensation of feeling such unity with that which they so love so dearly. It is natural to stop and experience feeling such grace, instinct intuitively knows it will be of great benefit to you. Fanatics are those that have spent much time in a belief, and not felt this love."

"The only way to aid them to feel, is to *be* the feeling," Amanda whispered. "That neutralizes the desire to blow us up again."

"So if we go to that church and just radiate this loving energy, you think it is going to neutralize hostilities?" Theresa inquired.

"No, not the four of us alone, but if we use our network to focus on the church, yes. Look, Peter and I have had this discussion many times. For decades upon decades the spiritual communities have been making claims of a new era, and New Age of enlightenment. Prophecies, predictions, processes, it has become a multibillion dollar business, does anyone truly believe that all those consumers are going to be willingly led into a life that will no longer require it? It posed the question to us, can we truly change with this easily and naturally, by responding to new and higher vibrations from the universe, as are appearing now? The old paradigm of pain and learning being synonymous is becoming repulsive to those embracing new energies," Sarah spoke with true authority.

Peter interjected, "If we focus energies into a particular area, can we alter the feelings being felt by the population within that area? Yes, we can to a very large degree. The opposite reality on a smaller scale would be a room of happy people being invaded by a very pissed off individual, the mood swing in the majority is instant, first fear, then anger.

"Sara and I explored deeply the idea of the reverse. Over the last few years, such focus has been pouring into that little Ohio town. The changes have been very present according to what Sarah has been sharing with me. The economy has rebounded, enrollment at the college is way up, with tuition reductions. Literally no one is on welfare or homeless anymore, and drugs and alcohol crimes are at a historic low for the last four decades. Fundamentalists, religionists are feeling the squeeze, the mud has been pushed back to them."

"They believe we teach heresy at the center, being as God. Teaching self healing, self evolving, self empowering. We are Satan's soldiers to them and many other religions. Their prophecies are interpreted to say this time would come, as a sign of the end, of course. But they built an escape clause for themselves into it. If you bring peace, and the world comes to a peaceful state, it will be the work of the Antichrist. It ensures the rain of fear to make the mud," Theresa added. "How would you respond to this, Peter?"

"I would say what I said in a pleasant talk with a priest. If I raised my being to the level of Jesus as you teach him, his abilities and sole connection to God, and all that he was, and said to you 'I am a true Son of God' just as he, would I still be anywhere near what God truly is? Does our spirit, mind, intelligence and heart, limit the reality of God? Because the truth of the vastness of our source is greater than we can think, imagine, or embrace. Even as a Christ."

Theresa smiled gently. "Good answer."

"I believe we're all ready to return now," Sarah said.

"I am returning also, I need to come out of this meditation and address things we have been discussing," Theresa piped up.

"Is so nice being in this space, seeing the universe so close and feeling it so deeply."

"Then bring it with you," Theresa advised. "Also, when you return, do not reenter your bodies too quickly. The Reiki aligners want to work you in slowly. There will be some physical pain from the blasts impact on your tissue and muscles, they will aid you in aligning slowly, a layer at a time."

IX
Healing

As our consciousness returned to the home of our bodies, we seemed to hover above them awhile, heeding Theresa's cautions. None of us looked too worse for the wear. I could see some minor bruising on myself, and Amanda, while Sarah had some pretty big ones on her face around her eyes. No surprises there though. When you get kissed by dynamite, walking away is a miracle unto itself. We seemed to be sleeping so peacefully, that it seemed a shame to wake us.

There were three people attending us in the room, two women I had seen earlier and a man I did not know. They were changing gauze cloths on our bruises, with what appeared to be an herbal mixture on the cloth. The door opened and Theresa and nine more people swarmed into the room with her.

"They are coming back into consciousness, now. Let's do this," she commanded.

I could see the orbs of consciousness align over Sarah and Amanda, and I began re-entrance into myself. I could feel myself lying just directly above my body, and there were four sets of hands around my body, two at each side, one at my feet, the last near my head. The energy from their hands extended outwards across my body, as if they were holding my energy body, and gently guiding me back in, slowly lowering someone into water. As I entered, it was a layer to layer feeling and imagery. I could see and feel each layer of skin as I passed through it and into the tissue, muscle and organs. They were lowering me a little at a time, adjusting at each layer, scanning for damage as my consciousness became aware of my bodies inner workings. Finally I was fully returned to my flesh. In meditation it is as if you are coming out of something, a sort of sleep, but not. This was the most gradual return to reality I had experienced, and the aid of others made it seem even more evolved. This was the old Reiki enhanced a thousand fold. Not only were the attending healers using their energies to lower me, they were smoothing out my energy as I entered into myself, like smoothing out the icing on a cake to conform to its curves and lines.

The woman at my head spoke to me. "Hello, Peter, welcome back and nice to meet you. I want you to hold a minute and let us work here for just a short bit. We're going to lift your energy body out again now that you have done your own scanning of your body and feel confident you're all right, then we're going to gently set you back in again in a single motion.

"This is a method of evolved energy alignment we have found allows the body and energy to be in a higher state of enhancement. It was developed for people coming to us that are in high states of anxiety and distress. It works very well for us and the people we deal with, but I cannot specifically say why. We just know it to work, and it will also aid in any pain from the impact you suffered."

It is like walking straight into a hurricane wind when a blast hits you like that. The mind scrambles to wrap around the event and seeks to know its damage level bodily. I let the people do what they were doing and cooperated fully. I had had Reiki treatments in the past, but this was a whole new level. I had never felt energy so profoundly from another's hands and with such solid support. I felt them lift me totally out again, and then reset me in. The feeling was amazing, as when you can finally crack your neck and you just feel it come back to its natural relaxed state.

"That was wonderful," I said.

"I am glad you enjoyed it, I feel you're going to be just fine. We would have liked you to sleep a bit more. But Theresa said we were lucky to get all of you to sleep this long. We have been doing energy healings on you around the clock, so you should be in good shape.

How do you feel?" she asked with a deep sincerity.

"I feel good, I truly do. I am aware of the bruising, but it is not painful," I said as I sat up. I looked over at Sarah and Amanda and they were already up and looking for clothing to wear. They were both walking around totally nude as they sought out their clothing around a room full of people. I noticed in this new energy I saw their bodies as something beautiful to behold, as a rare flower you would happen upon in a walk you expected to be mundane from familiarity with the surroundings. I felt no arousal at seeing the young women naked, no erotic inklings appeared in my mind, only wonder at the human form and the amazing design of it.

I remember reading in the Gospel of Thomas, Jesus talking of arousal being a choice within love, and when we could gaze at the naked body without knee jerk arousal appearing, then we would understand. The kingdom of Heaven is an earthly experience as was this moment of enlightenment. In higher states of awareness, nudity is a thing of beauty and admiration, not a thing of desire and want.

I however am old school. Holding my sheet, I asked where my clothes were.

"A little shy there, Peter?" Amanda said. "Think of it as being in a hospital, essentially it is, just a new form of it."

I could hear Sarah and some others in the room chuckling to themselves. After wrestling with the sheet and my clothes, I finally just lost the sheet to frustration. I felt very natural as well, and no one seemed to notice it anyway.

After finishing dressing, we all thanked everyone for their help and expertise, then they left and the four of us were alone again, this time in bodies. I sat on the edge of the bed looking out of a window into the park across the street, it was a beautiful day of sunshine, and people in the park with little ones running in the grass. Kind of a post card scene, and a direct contradiction of people blowing up. "It is what it is," I whispered to myself.

Theresa came over and put her hand on my shoulder. "Are you all right?"

"Yes, quite actually. I was just looking at the Norman Rockwell scene in the park and thinking of the explosion. Contrast is an interesting teacher. I was also feeling something familiar about the way I came back into my body, as if I had done it that way before, slowly and methodically, pausing to readjust when I felt it important to do so."

"It was the way we came back in as children after an abusive episode," said Sarah. "I recall it vividly, even feeling hands guiding me and a soft voice telling me how to heal as I went. I thought they were angels helping me then."

"Do you still think it was angels?" I asked.

"Yes, I just see angels differently now. I feel when we require the assistance of angels, I envision a group of light particles coming together and forming an angel, the form will be whatever we believe they look like. Some think of them as humans, others as winged women and men. I suppose everyone sees them as something different. But the light is what soothes, comforts, and conveys the wisdom to us. I realize that takes a lot the romantic vision of angels out of the equation, but for me it is an idea I can work with more readily."

"The experiences of being realigned in that new way made me think of my body, and of angels. I see angels as you do, something that forms for the response to human need and desire. But the body, I sensed harbors a resentment. For the most part we are taught it is a 'thing' a tool, vessel, any way you choose to phrase it. Religion puts it at war with spirit, and we think of it as something expendable in the end, waste material after death. But there is more to it, more it can feel and sense of its own power to do so. Does anyone else feel this?"

"I do, I have always felt that too," Amanda offered in.

"Referring to 'my body' as if I had bought it in a store somewhere, but it is the child of the mind. In the womb mind built it with spirit and intelligence. I always felt it was given really bad PR, especially by the current standard of its care. New reality dictates that it can according to design be as much a part our infinite life as soul."

Theresa was standing there with her hand on her chin obviously conforming words to her thoughts. "We are emerging from the Dark Ages of spirituality now. All that can be tried, resurrected, and configured from our spiritual beginnings is here in the present. We give them different titles every few years to refresh the market of buyers, but still, we have been on a treadmill of spiritual impotence for quite a few centuries. Churning our minds depths for some deep secret from the past that will suddenly catapult us into divine existence. I feel no matter what we find inside the pyramids, it just does not apply anymore, the human race has changed its geometry and the frequencies that operated the old temples does not work in our time, we are the new temples, everyone. We are the sacred space of Earth, or not. Our bodies march to the tune of a different drummer, the old religions are coming of age, and the human race is emerging from its adolescence into full maturity, but the dark age of spiritual superstition is not going to go quietly into the night it would appear."

"Our bodies are our Akashic records, the sacred repository of knowledge and wisdom so many seek under the ground. No one sees clearly how it will all play out, but yes, our bodies deserve to be seen as deeply Sacred as our souls. One and one, being one, not mind, body, and soul, not anymore," said Sarah.

"Well. We can settle this later." Theresa seemed anxious to get back to her plans. "I think we need to deal with our mole first, then seek out the lineage of our bomber's puppet master, perhaps we'll be doing both simultaneously. I will be in the child find section. I make Angie nervous, join me there in about twenty minutes while I prime the emotional pump."

"How cloak dagger of you, Theresa," Sarah said. "We'll be there."

Theresa swooped back out of the room with the unbroken stride of a figure skater. It's her style, moving in and getting directly to the point, and then gone again, but always leaving something worthwhile in her wake. There is no wasted motion in this place, no wasted energy because it is never taken for granted. There is an unspoken but always present statement in the motion of these people that says human life is sacred, not just valued.

The focus is on making the new and old paradigms work together until it is all new again without the historical mass destruction before building new designs of evolutionary thinking and courageous exploration of human genius. The root word for genius is genuine, and that's what is growing, a genuine social structure, that allows the individual to grow into full potential from their own perception of what that may be.

"Well, I guess we're all lucky to be here at all. I feel bruised but not anything like I thought I would be. When the blast hit me I thought it was over. I remember seeing your face, Amanda, and feeling grateful if that was going to be the last thing I saw. Peter, what can I say?"

"Say we can eat. I am starving, unless lunch was supposed to be gravel with wood chips in a dust sauce. In which case I'll eat elsewhere and join you later," I said, addressing them both.

"I am sure we can find something that you can eat. I am famished also. How about you Amanda?"

"I could definitely eat. We can go by the kitchen on the way to meet Theresa and address Angie's concerns with us. Only unknowns are feared, so let's tell her anything she wants to know," Amanda said as she headed for the hallway, with us falling into step. "I am going to stop by the child find wing, I will meet you two in the kitchen."

Sarah walked over to her and hugged deeply and kissed her ever so lightly on the cheek, then walked over to me. I knew we were heading for the great room.

"Amanda and Theresa like you very much, Peter. I am glad this is turning out to be a valuable trip for all of us it would seem."

"Yes, valuable learning experience. I am glad I came too. What are we looking for when we get there?"

"I am not sure, I just know we'll find it. I need to walk it calmly and feel what's still there to feel. Theresa and I have talked many times about stopping this sort of violence, and how to change the angry energies. We concluded that since historically those energies have always been with the human race, changing them ceased to be an option of any sense, but redirecting it was. The energy is there, it is inherit in human life. Action speaks the language of intent, defining the energy force, the velocity, if you will, of the emotion.

"Good and bad, the light versus the dark is the treadmill. Humanity stops moving to live the struggle of needing to resolve it. The yin yang is a stop sign, moving in a circle gets you nowhere. We are designed to feel, the result of chakras harmonizing. The more in harmony, the greater energies we can feel, it is our truest sight. This is where we redirect ourselves into the energies that far surpass light speeds, but we call it the calm."

"Yes, after meditating as long as I have, one comes to realize the illusion so often mentioned was actually within ourselves, that calm is a place of very rapid moving energies, that peace is a still point of non activity, and perfection is an ending to a goal. These are the illusions we deceive ourselves with mostly. Human beings are designed to function best when in motion. When the mind is thinking, spirit is moving and spirit lives in motion. A mind meditating is exploring states of extreme motion and activity, the meditator is the zero point of calm most meditators are seeking. Spirituality is stuck in its healing modality, stopped in its tracks until everyone is healed before things can occur in their philosophies, but beneath this thinking is judgment. I am healed, you are not."

"We have people here called healers, they cared for us. They understand energy and its relation to the human body, but always see that the body cures itself, they only provide energy, they do not tell it what to do once it leaves them and enters another. When a bone is broken, the doctor sets it, and the energy people provide the medicine of energy, and the bone mends much more quickly. Just as resetting us in our bodies aligned in a way we do not fully understand, but know it works to enhance us. We know it works to calm the children torn by a life of abuse, and those just too stressed out to find peace of mind. Peace of mind is not sitting on a beach to most, it is seeing where you desire to go in life, and moving towards it."

"I agree, Sarah. So what are you feeling in here?"

"I am feeling the source of this is someone at the church she attended, that she believed she would be addressed as a martyr even if she lived, because she was not expecting to die. The dynamite was never supposed to go off, it wasn't even wired to a detonator, not to mention that dynamite is a rather crude bomb anymore. Whoever sent her, shot her from a distance to blow her up, her shock and horror still permeate the energy here. The shooter was on the roof across the street. What are you getting, anything?"

"Yes, a bad memory. You know the energy of this place better than I, but I am definitely feeling a simple plan gone wrong. She wanted to stop this place, but not with murder. I keep getting an image of someone with power lost, deep anger for a perceived wrong done to him. Any ideas with that?"

"Yes, which is why we're going to the funeral in a few

hours. Wow, Theresa really has this place almost back together. They must have hit this place like a swarm of bees to get so much done. There must be a dozen Amish buggies out there, which means that there is great food being cooked, let's eat!"

"Right behind you."

X
Questions, Always the Questions

Sarah and I headed out for dinner, back down the old hallways of the cathedral looking for the kitchen. As we walked I could feel the ones that walked these halls so many years past. There lingered an air of sacredness that its occupants had considered abandoned by the world, beginning the transition of this place into a community problem instead of a place of prayer and sanctuary. The robed figures of its creation still haunted it in a respectful sort of way.

"Something is smelling very good, Peter. It's making my mouth literally water here," Sarah's said as her pace visibly picked up.

"Yes indeed. There were Amish living near the place I raised my children. They would come into town and sell their pies and cakes, cookies and other assorted foods. They would be sold out in a couple of hours. But it was worth the stopping for, believe me."

"I want to eat some, not talk about it, let's move it here." She was sprinting by now and finally we hit the kitchen, where she literally slid into the counter where the food was.

"Jesus, woman, haven't you ever eaten before?" I kidded.

"Yes, but this is treat time, my friend. Do you see Amanda?" she asked.

"Ah, yes, she is over there with some of the people that were with us in the room a little while ago. She just saw you. You know Sarah. Her eyes light up when she sees you."

"I know, and mine do the same. We are more than lovers, Peter, so much more I believe. She is always talking to me in my head. Sometimes I have to tell her to give it a rest though, like now. I know you can sense the chatter, I have been feeling

Theresa talking with you that way since we returned."

"That she has been. You know it's a real time saver though, being able to communicate on different levels at the same time. Theresa and I have been getting acquainted and still doing other things without interference."

"I find it's very much like the Internet, we have IM dialoguing, then psychic mail, like e-mail we open it when we have the time, along with the ability to communicate globally. The Internet is actually a very ancient design, but with this, we do not have to worry about power loss, no calamity can stop the communications. Since developing this within myself and others, computer time is minimal. Even the computers in the child find project are mostly for location now, the psychics are in touch with the children from find to rescue anymore."

"Young children are very open and will hear well internally. They are more focused inside than out, explaining why I was always saying their name three times before I got 'HUH?' from them."

"They were lucky to have you for a father, Peter."

"I don't know about that, I was learning then more than practicing my beliefs. They went through some very rough times with me. They saw and heard things I would take back in a second if I could, but I cannot. I owe them more than they will ever realize. I love them with all my being, because they taught me how to love. Do you want help with that plate, or should I just retrieve a cart for you?"

"Very funny. I will work out tonight, there are exercise classes going on here all the time, any kind you can think of, and a really nice weight room too. Martial arts and yoga are a constant here as well. This place is jumping after dark. I am friggin' starving."

"Yeah, I can tell."

"Keep it up, if it takes an explosion to get food like this, then we're going to have a lot more of them. The Amish are probably the most misunderstood people in the U.S. We retrieved a couple of young girls that were kidnapped. When they returned them home to them, they were openly happy and grateful, but equally concerned with the couple that stole them. They could not have kids, and it was a crime of opportunity. They are in jail and the community writes to them weekly, even the mother of the girls. Forgiveness is more than words to them."

"I knew some personally, indeed they are good people, and with a great sense of humor too I found. So, is Theresa married?"

"Where did that come from?"

"Just curious, she's an intriguing woman. Very stoic in appearances and the way she carries herself, but I sense a heart of pure gold."

"Your senses are entirely correct. It was she, Amanda and I that got this running. She was our physics professor. She also taught classes on meditation techniques and spiritual principles. But the class that bonded us was one offered on attaining the positive developments an abusive experience can awaken in a person. Using the negative energy for positive result is how abuse is survived. The longer the experience the greater the development. An abuser over a period of time creates their own demise in the ones they abuse. Slave masters create rebels. A genius appears in the intelligence, awakening an epiphany, discovering a knowing that shows the way to maneuver and navigate it. If you live in a mine field, the first order of business is to become immune the explosions. Then there is nothing to manipulate, step on the mines and keep walking, then look at truth in their faces."

"Theresa taught you how to live alive. I am assuming this will be the topic at the funeral."

"I don't know. I rarely prepare things, I just do them I guess. But before I do I will do a light workout, then sit on my knees with hands together in deep meditation. It just feels so good to be really close to the silence, it makes me happy. By the way, she is married, but separated."

"Yes, me too. It remains about heart, that feeling that seems to make me feel full into every atom. Feeling a water misting in a hot summer day, then hitting a breeze with all your being. As a boy I learned 'God is love' and it took me half a century to know what it feels like. After you learn that you do not have to live unpleasantly by someone else's hands, we do not have to from ourselves. Then I learned immunity was to radiate love that strongly, fear doesn't pass its threshold. I use to feel safe in buildings like this as a child, I felt God's house was a place negativity would not survive in. Now I know I felt safe in the feelings I felt there. Even then my response to religion was 'Just Say No.'"

"But the truth is, most religious people feel about their perception of God as we do when in that deep meditation, close, loving, and that deep feeling of being caressed with love and wisdom, and that is the common ground for us all. That is the ground of sacred essence, human beings in the common natural state. The place where genius comes from, to create, invent, discover and expand. None of us have ever found the vocabulary for it in any history, you have to know it."

There is something inherently good about eating and talking, food and ideas seem to go together deeper than social graces and habit stored in DNA for future tradition. Eating, purging, talking, are all human requirements that ignore class distinctions or perception of differences, we are kin in this realm of humanness.

Amanda was busy talking with the healers that tended all of us. She was an information sponge always asking, always seeking to know. As we all are, be it deep spiritual and scientific knowledge or the latest gossip, human beings are seekers of information.

Sarah finished her pie, inhaling it like Jell-O off a plate. "We have to meet Theresa in a few minutes here. Amanda is staying here to finish then heading back to the child find area. She doesn't feel it important for her to be there. So let's rock, we have wasted enough energy on this explosion of ours." Her voice carried a definite "done with this mess" tone as she spoke the words.

We headed back through a couple hallways and stepped into the room Theresa favored for talks, the plain one with the grand chair she sat in as before. Angie was there already talking with Theresa. The air was congenial and casual feeling, light conversation was all they had exchanged.

"Hi, Sarah, I am glad you're all right," she said, standing. "You must be Peter. I recognize you from slamming into me in the hallway. Not the best way to met people." She was shaking my hand, looking me up and down as she did. She was a person that accessed people with her eyes, seeking out details in their eyes, postures, and subtle body movements, she was all about her training and procedure.

"It is a pleasure, and sorry about slamming into you all back there, didn't have a real choice, but everyone is fine, that's what matters to all of us," I said as I pulled my hand back.

"Yes, it is. Well, what's this meeting about? I think we're about to find a child back there today, I know we're very close," she said.

Theresa began, "We were just wondering what you are telling the Cleveland office when you report back to them? We know that you are doing so in detail. What is it that you and they are expecting to find here?"

"All right, we may as well be open if we're putting our cards on the table here."

"Good," Theresa said, "we will tell you anything you desire to know about us. You have been working with us about a year, so there is a lot you already know. But you suspect we are more than what we appear?"

"I did when I came here, as did Cleveland. I actually came in to see why suddenly so many missing kids were being found through here. We knew our agents weren't just out in the field looking and miraculously finding them. Surely you understand the curiosity. For all we knew you could have been connected to the disappearances."

"What do you know then about the bombing?" Sarah asked.

"Not much more than you actually. We know the church is very fundamentalist, and that the pastor is the old mayor, the one you displaced when he lost the election to your husband, Theresa. He had been the mayor here forever until this place opened."

"Indeed he was," Sarah countered. "I remember as I came here the first time on a bus, the billboard just outside of town read 'This Is Jesus Country' with a huge picture of Jesus on it. This is a very conservative Christian town, with a very liberal arts college in it, so the contrast was here when I arrived. The college is a moneymaker for the town though, so differences are overlooked in that regard."

"My husband and I are separated, but that isn't anything relative to the fact he won because he bypassed the traditional avenues of election and took his proposals directly to the voters, told them in a real plan for the city how we wanted to redirect it to more growth. It wasn't promises without facts, figures and a plan they could read for themselves. It was something they could read at the dinner table, and say, yes this could work, or no I don't think can."

"Irregardless," Angie continued. "The upset was a real blow to him and to the church. I think he talked that woman into this plan to intimidate the center. What went wrong from there is still to be seen."

Sarah broke in here. "Does your Cleveland office believe we are some subversive group here, stealing children for profit? Planning to overthrow the government?"

"They think you have an unnatural ability to find these kids too easily," she replied. "They know our agents come here to gather information and get the facts they need to return these kids home. They have profilers, psychics with degrees in criminology that do not get the results this place has."

"I think the ex mayor is behind the explosion, but do not trust that he wasn't working on someone else's behalf as well. It's a pretty bold move for having lost an election in a backwater town in Ohio," I added.

"True, but this little town was his empire," she said with confidence. "He lost a lot and hadn't lost before. In his mind I am sure he lost this town and Jesus is not happy about it, to a bunch of New Age psychics with new ideas and the devil's ideas at that. I know the initial call to Cleveland came from him two days after the election. He reported that FBI agents were coming here, and that they were into things he was sure the office should know about."

Sarah stood up. "Well I have dealt with this long enough, the explosion is done, everyone is fine, except the woman, and I think you're wrong about the son, all of you. I feel he shot her, not knowing she was wearing a dynamite belt. When I confronted him outside that other morning, he wanted to kill her, it was his only vision of freedom in his mind, I saw it clearly. I think the old mayor is sitting at home peeing himself because this all got so out of hand. I also believe Angie, you are in agreement with your home office, that we are not quite kosher in our intent for this place. So here we all are. You have been coming here for nearly a year now, you have been snooping into the dynamics of us all, and tell us, what have you concluded?"

"I have concluded nothing, Sarah. I cannot decide on any of this. The home office is all over my case to produce something that will explain it, but what am I going to report, that there are a bunch of people living in Ohio that can find missing children with some ancient voodoo method of criminology? That people are being healed by hands-on energy freaks, yet I cannot deny the reality of what I see. It's making me crazy sometimes to even think of it. I can't even sleep at night."

"I am sorry this all causes you so much distress, Angie. I truly am. But life is changing all around the world, and there is no real way to write it out in a report the FBI will swallow, or any security organization for that matter, none. It's not about any of that though, it's about finding theses kids and the method isn't even important as far as we are concerned. It's just what we do here, and will continue to do. But I will say this, the Cleveland office will see it firsthand because our next center will be there. Ohio is a broke state. Cleveland is the number one poverty city in the union. Columbus is the capital city that is breaking this state's economy. The taxes on every person in this state are outrageous, college tuition is one of the highest in the country, and corporations are being driven out by unbending politicians refusing tax breaks to stay here. This is one of the most corrupt states going."

"So what then, you're going to turn all that around?" Angie asked. "Some young college graduate fresh out of school? We know about the old man five years ago, Sarah. We know he was autopsied and he did not die from a stroke or heart attack. Witnesses put you and Peter there that day. We know people are dying and that you are there when they do. What do you expect us to think?"

"I do not expect anything. I do not intend to be deterred either. The world is always screaming about its problems, its woes, and freedom from tyranny. Well their prayers are being answered, not by 'some young college graduate' but by the millions that are as we are here. It does not matter if we are working together in a center, or just living in a suburb raising a family, people are evolving, not generation to generation, but every moment they focus on it. You're not blind, you see it, feel it, and desire it too, I can feel that. Everyone that died did so by their own choice. A serial molester died that morning, and a woman that was so blinded by faith she actually thought putting on dynamite would end with some sort of victory, so focused on pleasing Jesus, she did not see her own son slipping into darkness. The secret is out, Angie, have you seen the movie yet? Because it is and never was a secret, but it has people believing in themselves, and that is what will change the world, not me or anyone here, yet me and everyone here."

"So you did not kill that old man?"

"How, Angie, think, from across a room? I gave him back his own shit, and it was so much he could not live with it either. Will you take that to a grand jury? Just as the son, will you arrest him, tell the prosecutor that he was known to be the shooter by a psychic that saw him killing his mother in his mind? Where is the hard evidence to put him on trial? Where is the evidence of our nationwide child stealing ring? It's not going to fly Angie, there is no wind beneath any of its wings. People die every day, Angie from real criminals, but there are none here."

Theresa stood also. "It is a new world out there, not in the coming anymore, but here. People have been changing all along the centuries, but now in our lifetime, they are changed. It is not just a spiritual progression, but a scientific one and an evolutionary one. Like it or not, believe it or not life is pro-human. The universe supports life on this little planet, and God however you perceive it, it is real. Something larger than us as a whole that has thoughts, feelings, and intelligence. What happened five years ago in some coffee shop to a man that molested children does not require the FBI's attention, it eliminates the need for it. That is the Cleveland offices fear, not some spiritual center here. If the sheriff actually cleans up the town, he eliminates the need for himself. What will cancer research companies do if it is stands cured and eradicated? Do not be so untrue to yourself as to not believe that our world's economies rely on crime, disease, and even disasters. If we run out of natural ones, we always have the nuclear ones to fill the gaps. If politicians decide on peace, there is always religious genocide."

"If I may offer some perspective here. It's not about old men in coffee shops getting what they created. It is about the world's issues actually being resolved. Sarah did not kill anyone; she purged herself of emotions that would have killed her, as did the kids at the graduation ceremony, granted those emotions would not have killed them, but they were in the way of ones that would enhance everyone's relationship. It is the way of it now. Humanity has lived in the struggle for so long, giving it up is actually more frightening than having their prayers answered," I offered.

"I am going to go meet Amanda and work out together. Angie, I thank you for being so honest. You need to do what is best for yourself and what makes you at peace with yourself as well. I see no reason to arrest the son. He is tortured enough, nothing anyone can do to him will cause him anymore grief than himself. I feel deeply sorry for him.

"The old man is a closed issue in my life. He was when Peter and I walked out of the coffee shop. We talked once about it and then moved on in our friendship, because we accepted the new is here now, and things will never be what they were, no matter how many people blow themselves up in the name of God. Religions that use violence to spread themselves, will die the same, for if no one else will war with them, they will kill each other, Iraq, Afghanistan, Somalia, here in the twin towers. When Gandhi freed India, they went immediately into civil war over God's true people, true religion, and true government. The way of the new is for people to take such responsibility unto themselves, for themselves.

"Govern yourself, develop your own relationship with whatever you believe, and cure yourself by prevention first and foremost. Healers here show everyone they can, they do not fear not being needed, they invite the reality, because they trust they will always be taken care of, and there will always be children learning."

"I have a lot to ponder I guess," Angie said. "I want to believe all this, but I know the world I live in, or at least I thought so. I don't know what the hell to tell Cleveland anymore."

"We can work on that later this evening, Angie," Theresa offered. "Go get something to eat, take a walk and forget it all for a while. You're welcome to keep working here and stay as long as you like."

"Thank you, Theresa."

"You're entirely welcome." She turned to me. "Would you like to walk with me awhile, Peter?"

"Yes, yes, I would, thanks. I could use it."

"Do you think she is lying, Peter?"

"No, I think she *is* a lie."

XI
Surreal Landscapes of the Mind

Sarah ran off to meet Amanda. They had not had time alone since the blast and were anxious to find it. Sarah walked slowly, mulling things over in her mind, she was thinking of what she was going to do/say when she got to the church this evening. This wasn't just a little Baptist church in the country. It had a congregation of over a thousand members, and was even televised the Sunday and Wednesday services. Theresa and her husband had been invited to a service during the election, with a televised debate of the issues after the service, she and Amanda had attended. She recalled the debate going very badly for the Mayor, and the whole service feeling like a staged production, with TV cameras moving up and down the main aisles. The pastor, one Otis Slusher, came out in a pure white suit, with a choir singing behind him, it was just two strippers away from a Vegas floor show.

But there was also big money flowing within this church, old money, money for the cause of Jesus.

Whatever she did, it better be good.

She finally came to the doors of the child safe room, pushed one open and entered. It was busy as always, she saw Angie in front of a monitor looking intently into its images, she said they were close to a find, she is here because she really does care what Sarah had sensed in the meeting, and this place "works" and that is her bottom line in anything she suspected. David and Karl came over to her and expressed happiness at her walking around, alive and well, then returned to their interests, they were cops through and through.

Just then Amanda caught sight of her, her face lit up and

they walked quickly to one another and embraced tightly, burying each other's faces into the neck of the other.

"Let's get out of here," Amanda whispered.

"I am with you," Sarah returned to her ear.

There are workouts, and there are "workouts" and the two disappeared out the doors together. As soon as they exited, they kissed deeply and passionately. It was time to be close, and to feel deeply. Love does not ask your beliefs if it can be expressed, it just moves you to act, to be human and feel it. True lovers can lie together in snow parkas and feel more intimate than skin to skin. Just presence in the same room can cause a connection felt by everyone. This is the connection between Sarah and Amanda. They can move and feel as one, yet remain fiercely independent in their lives.

Sensuality and sexuality, far cries from the ability of human beings to be intimate. It is easy to take off one's clothes and be sexually open. To kiss so deeply into one another's spirits that one cannot tell in truth where one leaves off and the other begins, a simple glimpse into the undulating lovemaking of the cosmos, the God and Goddess entwined in everlasting procreation of creation. Sarah and Amanda fell into one another when they embraced, without restriction and reservation of what one may find in the others mind and heart.

They returned to their room. They had laid claim to three rooms that shot upward forming the tower of the great structure. A spiral staircase connected ground level to the upper rooms, all the way to the pyramid shaped room holding the ancient bells that had been silent for so long. Sarah and Amanda felt the room to hold a sacred energy from the years the bells had sent their Mantric tones out across the countryside. Weather permitting, they used it to meditate in and a place they often made love together.

They showered together as soon as they reached their privacy. Clothes lay in a heap to allow revelation of desire to be seen and felt, they stood under the warm water in a face to face embrace, skin seeking skin, tongues entwined, nipples hardening in search for connection, it was the dance of the ancients in the heart of the young. Love pouring from one to the other as their skin reached for it as ravenous travelers finally finding the feast of an inn only royalty dined within. The force of their love overpowered the skins ability to drink and feast on the others, Love all encompassing becomes reality destroying childhood fairy tales of such feeling and emotion in light of power that makes the body a tool of expression and not the focus. As they pressed closer than possibility allowed, orgasms exploded into the watery realm, mixing nectar and honey in the mind's desire for the heart to know itself and another in the same flow from within, acts of Love within sensuality that angels would fall for from their lofty heights to feel just once.

They recovered their sense of reality long enough to towel off and adjourned to the bed, where hours more of divine touch and unbridled passion drained them of all nectar and power to resist sleep, knowing fully, awakening would find them light years beyond renewed, walking in the truth of rejuvenation, essence sleeping with essence cradled in the arms of angels.

In this new ideal of interconnectedness being a real time truth, such powerful feeling cannot be secluded into the mind of one or two, it moves along a wind no one sees, yet all feel. Some know its truth, while others just want to smile for seemingly no reason at all, just because something had entered them that feels good, beyond its known definition.

For some, it is a feeling of not feeling anger in that moment, or depression takes a momentary sabbatical from consciousness to remind one of what feeling good was like, so they may choose to recapture its wholeness. Still others feel a stirring to find their partners of choice and make love with them, carrying a nagging seed that it can lead to a deeper closeness than sex normally allows, that sex holds a secret within its act, a portal to intimacy that would somehow even eliminate itself from the equation of human relationship, that orgasm was only a map to a greater delight in human expression and feeling.

Sex to the ancients was divine touch in human form, to those that elevated themselves to not drinking from the water with full face into the stream as the animals did. They had known to cup their hands and drink as a human beings, even in intimacy. They had become acutely aware that a seed was within them that could give new life to another human, and a seed within the seed would birth God upon the Earth within generations of patience and trust. While in the mind of the animal human, sex was but a method for dispelling the desire to kill and to possess, to fight and harm, it somehow tamed the emotions of the survival dominance of human life. Even unto this day and time we see it still being used for such primitive desires, an ignorant understanding that some deep hunger is fed within the human minds misunderstanding of sexual purpose and desire. Rape is the act of ravenous starvation, committed by both male and female in our time. It will not cease until we teach the poor to feed themselves with the Manna of Heaven, the energy of the universe that truly sustains us in life.

Amanda awoke to find the bed empty of Sarah, nothing new, but how sweet it would be to roll over and pull her close before rising for life. She knew where she was, in the bell tower looking into the sky, seeing what only she could see, hearing what only she could hear.

Amanda arose and jumped into the shower again, seeing the evidence Sarah had already done so. While in there, she thought to the psychics in the child find room and inquired if the girls had been returned to their homes, they had. It bought a smile to her face and a breeze of love into her heart.

Sarah stood looking ever upward and outward into the sky. Her thought had long since left the atmosphere and was deep into the universe's privacy. It was so natural to feel as intimate with such vastness as even the confined area of her own room. A friend of infinite size and power that held no fear in its unknown galaxies. Her mind shifted to the ancient teaching of the Quaballah she had read so long ago, that each person was a universe unto themselves. Peter had helped her understand that this was not a metaphorical thing, but quite literal. When meeting each new person in our life we are entering a very real universe as we converse with them. Each person is God of that realm, and as responsible for it as the great intelligence of the macro universe is responsible for the one she floated her consciousness in at this very moment.

It is hard at times for the mind to wrap around the idea of mortality and immortality being a choice of human will and insight, but it is. Knowing at some point the universe she was embracing would one day be gone, that Earth would someday be only a myth, a story of the planet of the God seed they had all been birthed from. Knowing too that she would be there and aware in that time also. Form does not matter, only the truth it is so, whatever form may be then.

Sarah gently reeled her mind back into the present moment as she heard Amanda's footsteps on the stairs. She turned to see her arising from the floor as she navigated each stair effortlessly. The light from beneath her arose with her, giving the illusion of her rising from the light itself. The mind reaches to such visions and moves into surreal desire, seeing the future in the present somehow, yet unwilling to loosen its grip on the belief of reality as solid ground.

Amanda came up next to her and stood there looking into the sky as well.

"That was beautiful last night, you are beautiful," she whispered into the sky's embrace.

"I know, Amanda, I truly know."

XII
The Elders

Theresa and Peter had left the center to walk around town. It seemed needed to put things back into perspective for them. As they passed through the entrance, the workers were busy restoring things to their original look.

"Sarah has wanted us to meet for some time now, Peter," she said while still examining the work.

"I know, she has told me of you right along. I felt very comforted in your acceptance of her and your guiding hand in her life here. I was concerned when she left for college. I know she had Amanda with her, but youth can always be impetuous and take risks often beyond ability of experience. Although we're not talking of your run-of-the-mill teenagers, are we?"

"No, we certainly are not. They were an inspiration to me, to everyone they touch. Yet they serve as a constant reminder, this is it, this is the new human being we are all becoming faster than we can even comprehend it. So much has changed so quickly, and the mind at one time raced beyond light speed to try and keep up, but somehow relaxed into understanding when it ceased trying to."

"We are standing in the face of our wildest dreams and deepest fears in the same mirror. It reflects everything in us, nothing hidden, nothing lurking in the gray areas any longer, there are no gray areas. The subconscious is an enormous 'now' with the answers open for the asking. It seems eons in the coming with only light years yet to go, then into infinity. At times I feel as a dinosaur here, and other times I feel like the newest life form in the universe. It's the old pendulum thing, and God how I hate that feeling," I said.

"I know, Peter, the old analogies of the pendulum and the roller coaster. It seems so long ago we used them with any real emotion, but brings up old feelings I delete immediately. There is just no point staying there, even for the sake of reminiscing. Remembering has a whole new connotation to it, actual remembering to something requires deep scrutiny of what emotions will occur when we do."

"You know, Sarah and Amanda are hoping we will 'hook up' while I am here. She was talking about you incessantly the week before I was to leave for here."

"Yes, matchmaking is a human characteristic that will never change in all likelihood. She has been playing you up for a while to me. Youth rarely 'gets it' about needs changing as we mature."

"I have been alone for a long while now, and I don't mind it at all. I was married, but I do like being single. I like getting up and just walking out of the house when I decide to. I like walking at whatever time of day or night I choose to. I like not sharing all my decisions or having to answer for things I choose to do. It gets lonely sometimes I guess, but there are always people that like to share wherever one goes in life, you just have to be willing to speak up."

"I have been separated for a couple of years from my husband, it was a mutual desire to live apart. We have a good relationship, we dropped the drama of it quickly, realizing it was mostly programming and fear from being married so long. Drama is the way people tear their energies apart, like unweaving a basket with extreme aggression. It can be done differently with extreme choice."

"I thought so, but some people will not override their programmed responses, even if their life was hanging in the balance, and it often is. The drama around the center is the same, the old is coming apart, unweaving, and the drama will be extreme within the old designs. Sarah, all the Sarahs in the world are in danger if we do not weave a new design with speed enough to contain the damage," I said.

"An analogy I would concur with. I know Sarah told you the next center is opening in Cleveland, but she didn't elaborate on the reality that it will take up a complete city block. We have acquired property in the older warehouse district, a bit of a rough neighborhood, but one we feel we can really work with. The older business districts are easier for us to adapt to, they are structurally sound and offer a lot of office spaces and an equal amount of large open rooms as well. We are ready for the next step into a new reality, and that is to work openly in a heavily populated area, under the noses of the FBI, and one of the largest medical centers in the country, The Cleveland Clinic. Although the medical community is heading for holistic and alternative approaches, it must be stopped from being 'Americanized' and by that we mean becoming so expensive people find themselves in the same sinking ship they are with traditional medicines. Once they gain control of alternative therapies and the herbal remedies, it will require prescriptions and the prices will multiply faster than a computer can calculate, and growing natural herbs will come under the controlled substances act making it illegal to cultivate privately."

"It is a double-edged sword. There are a lot people out there practicing alternative medicines and healing doing more damage than good, and a lot more people taking herbs with limited knowledge of what they are taking. Many of the herbs in the larger chain stores are imported from overseas, with some of them you're lucky to get even one percent of the actual herb in the capsule, the rest are fillers from grass to even ground animal bone in some. Without regulation and certifications the doors are wide open for frauds, but when they are implemented, pricing is wide open," I said.

"Health is going to have to evolve into a personal responsibility, with prevention of illness the only way out of the traps set out there. That's where we have played such an impact full role here in this sleepy little town. The university is a place of education, and we have just carried it outside its doors, into the streets. A lot has changed here since we opened the centers doors. Originally this was a religious college, but economics caused it to 'lower' its acceptance standards to qualify for federal funding," Theresa said with a congenial smile, she really was a beautiful woman.

"Things began to really take off when Sarah returned from her summer apprenticeship in Brazil her first year here. She was so passionate about things, so hyped up about opening a center here. She was working at a new hospital Brasilia, studying intuitive diagnosis. It was an amazing place as she described it, a state funded hospital that staffed specialists in meditation, intuitive diagnosticians, herbalists, even psychics working alongside standard psychologists. She returned amazed by the insight by the country to deal with medical issues in such an open and experimental way, and equally disgusted by the practices here in the States. She was determined to inundate this town to what she had seen there."

"Yes, she often emailed me from there, her enthusiasm was contagious, even over the Internet the energies poured from her. I have a friend that studied in Peru in a similar atmosphere, she eventually moved there and is staffed in a hospital there as an intuitive as well, here she was a psychic working the fairs and barely scratching out a living, but there she is a respected member of the staff. Odd one has to go to a third world country to be respected for such abilities," I said disdainfully.

"When we decided to put this center together we talked long into many nights. We decided the first order of business was not clean up other establishments, but to clean up our acts as 'spiritual' people. The very term spiritual has been so misused and worn to death it has little to no potency any longer. The most important change was that we had to become a formidable force of change, we had to produce the boasts made."

"The shift to self-awareness was the key, self being the operative word."

"Yes, self was the key all right. Even us old-timers, like ourselves, had to realize we had given so much of our power away, we were about to become extinct like our religious ancestors. Over the years so many isms, osophies, and New Age bullshit movements came down the road, 'the Path' had become impassable. I was so into improving myself, I lost myself in all of it. It was where my husband and I lost one another, only emerging to discover we had no clue who we were any longer. We separated to rediscover ourselves, then decided we were not people that wanted to live together any longer. No hate, no anger, just a sensible understanding."

"Been there, done that. Seems we're always into recreation of ourselves, so how can anyone know who they are living with? If you're partnered with someone that does not change at all, it makes you crazy and you make them crazy. People want change, as long as it does not create changes. But life is changing, and at a pace we can't imagine, because it is happening beyond our ability to imagine, to think, to comprehend a final picture of it. It is never finished."

"Well put, my new friend. We seek new in everything that we do, yet have deep ties to the old. Time does not truly exist, so it is all relative. I notice you do not wear a watch."

"No, I haven't worn one most of my life. There are enough clocks around, and I can feel what time it is pretty closely. I use to work outside, and you learn to tell it by the sun, or relearn I think is more accurate. Einstein was right, time is a theory, and one not really relevant to much we do in life, except to get to work on time. Civilization seems measured by its restrictions of motion during the twenty four hour frame, accountability of actions performed within the structured times."

"People seem to feel uneasy with free time. Free and open space makes humans nervous, feeling vulnerable, and suspect. Too many generations of being controlled and sequestered in their busyness. Such is the present in the old ways, now is quite different. Things are moving rapidly enough that the mind only senses it on a very deep level. Keeping its secret until the biology aligns and consciousness can allow its presence," she said.

Theresa spoke with an authority that emanated confidences of things born of a future we have note seen yet. Yet her speech made one look for them in the light of the current day.

To see clearly what was truly transpiring here, it took a release of reality perceptions, and let the mind wander out into an evolution of its own freedoms. Like a laser shooting out into space, and being able to see where it traveled and also seeing clearly from whence it came. It is often said "today's fiction is tomorrow's reality" but this is today's fiction being today's reality.

We were walking casually now through a quiet town, old buildings stating to the great monolith of education it should not forget its roots, that genius grows on farms long before it enters a university to realize they are genius.

Theresa and I were "old guard" having come through the darker ages of this new emergence into light. Although the term light had become associated with divine presence, it was still a literal translation in the present. Light meant simply that, what was once hidden in darkness or secrecy was now walking in the light of day, "there it is" you can say, in your face. We knew how to work in the gray, to move about freely within beliefs designed to keep people small within themselves, living primordially within their fears of basic survival skills, supplying a never-ending stream of "things" to emulate growth as individuals, family units, and populations. We were living amongst the "day walkers" in this humble town of Ohio, networking with thousands of such places around the world.

It was clear that the youth would carry us into the unknown that has been predicted for so many centuries. We of the Elders were here out of a respect for having done the trench work, risen to this new height of human evolution by sheer determination and self disciplines, down the many roads and paths carved out of the hardest of granite in the human mind to believe in its animalistic natures. All the Sarahs in the world were now uniting as a global empathic entity. I recalled a scripture from youth about all things coming to light, everything being known. The normal rebelliousness of youth has become an imperative part of the equation for the new formula. The news reports only the youth that screams loudly in their frustration, while the Sarahs sought the cloak of self-awareness and self-education in the ways of the evolved human. In the new paradigm lies are not possible, deception becomes impotent, and corruption is instantly self-destructive.

As in the coffee shop, the lies were self-revealing, had Sarah desired to stop the process, she could not have, she had the courage to go with a power within her stronger than herself, emerging from the experience beyond any defining ideal of strength.

I said to Theresa, "I am an observer, and as we have been walking I see a plan unfolded. All the city's planters along the streets are a combination of herbs and flowers. As well as most of the landscaping at the university. I see people freely cutting them and the elderly tending them, quite an impressive thing in these times."

"It was all planned in a co-operative effort between the university's students and the centers people. Students use the town as their senior thesis, to come up with a new direction for the economy of it, the farms, and the business. We bypassed the current city administration and took the plans directly to the voters at the council meetings, and the university radio and TV stations broadcast it to the voters, as well as local town meetings. It is how my ex became the mayor and the old one from the church was replaced after twenty some years. The students in the horticulture programs went out to the farms and sat down with each farm owner and their families and showed them ways to increase their profits with herbal growing and exporting, and new farming designs for larger regular crops as well, also converting them over to tilless farming for natural fertilizing, cheaper and more effective for consumer and environment. There were so many changes on so many fronts we could not keep up with it. Turn imagination and intelligence loose and stand back for the genius."

"I can see why there is so much anger within the old regimes and why the center is so targeted. Damn hippies!"

Theresa laughed out loud. "We plan the same strategies in Cleveland, as it has some of the finest universities in the country, but all hurting economically."

"Might have something to do with the reality that Ohio colleges are some of the most expensive in the country as well."

"You think? Ohio has taxed its population and business right out of the state, you think they would have learned from the same mistakes in the twenties and thirties when they drove all the big money out to New York. New days, new methods, and new navigation into yet another unknown for the human race. Peter, let's talk like a couple of old empaths from the trenches here for a moment, shall we?"

"Works for me, what's on your mind?"

"The explosion, Sarah will not focus on it, but we are not fully into this new paradigm, and as we know, the transition is dangerous, from small town governments to the entire global picture. Unity will bring massive energy shifts as the global groups form a new matrix within the old mass consciousness, but much of the population is not aware of themselves, and they are the ones with the most radical and deadliest philosophies of change and conversion. The war with Islam and Christianity is about wealth, monetary and energy, wealth by control of the populations, nothing new. The energies are finding the people of sincerity within all beliefs, but those of no beliefs except self preservation will sense this as a deep attack on the status quo. Retaliation will be severe as we are seeing now within religious people."

"I think it is more fear than retaliation. Prophecy is the core of religion, always keeping fruition off in a distant future, attainable, yet not. Catholicism created the ultimate manipulation by making a reward of being controlled in the present, to attain heaven only after death. The congregations have begun falling away and prophecy fulfillment is needed to bring them back. Fear, such as 9/11 brought them back temporarily, but soon we forget.

"But if the apocalypse could occur, and the great Jihad, then once again the world would worship as it is told, for having brought this destruction upon itself. Christians are running scared of themselves, and Islam is creating Jihad to avoid westernization of it at all cost, with its worst fear being people that think for themselves. Only infidels and whores think their own thoughts and take responsibility for them."

"We, you and I, are a couple of old empaths, that have honed their skills enough to read large populations as individuals. It is not so hard to read a large body of human beings within the same thought frames. Like minds form a like mind, a single thought if you will.

"Sarah is the next step in the evolution, yet we are all equal in this empathetic motion of humanity. The old ways condense the energies of people until they are forced to seek new thinking, or allow their demise, the flaw in the plan was they take out potential with them when they explode. Sometimes the most apparent display is the subtle one being sought. Hide it where everyone can see it, and it goes unnoticed as a part of the scenery of human routine." Theresa spoke her words with strength and assurance.

"Empath is a word for the new millennium. When we were learning to refine those skills, we were just different, shunned, and feared. But, that was then and this is now. The importance of these evolved arts and sciences is what we put into the atmosphere of energy, not what we sense in them so much. Our filters are well established and meditation skills allow us to draw our life blood from a pure source, the source. Yet toxic energies abound like polluted waters, with the same result. People are only seeing clearly the need to feed the energy body with emotions of purity and wellness. Religion will play itself out, but the closer to the end of the play, the more enemies they will imagine and conjure into others beliefs. Meditation is now a state of being, and psychic is a state of living, both have evolved. As the human evolves, so to do their tools."

"Sarah is going to the church this evening, and I know she feels it is time to hit the ground running with all this. She will playback the emotion of them into their own minds, it is what empaths do, especially the new versions of them. It is the light on the side of the hill that illuminates the whole valley, just as the Pyramid cap stone did. In that church there will be no dark corners to lie from, no escaping what anyone feels."

"Welcome to now," I said.

"Shall we go meet the 'ladies' and help them unleash hell?" Theresa said with a sly smirk.

XIII
Hell Unleashed

"I sense Theresa and Peter are on their way back here," Sarah said to Amanda.

"Do you think they liked one another?"

"If they both return alive, it was a hit. Peter is an enigma, I know a lot about him, but not a lot really about 'him' but Theresa is the same I suppose. I know they will work well together, but they are both of the times that require their times of seclusion, time to be alone with themselves. Most around here chalk it off to being Elder, but it is something quite different with them both. Sometimes I would not hear from Peter for a month, then I would get an email like he had spoken to me yesterday."

Amanda walked over to Sarah and wrapped her arms about her waist, resting her chin on her shoulder. "Yes, Theresa has her 'unavailable' times also, it makes everyone crazy when she cannot be found."

"True, but she told me once, she sometimes does that when too many seek her for troubleshooting. She desires self education, but be assured, she is well aware of what is transpiring. It is no accident she appears in the doorway as disaster looms," Sarah whispered in Amanda's loving embrace.

"Peter would always know when I was in trouble also. Although we are good at the immediate response with people in our lives, we truly need to learn the distance sensing they do, and the way they can feel an entire country's emotions like they were standing in a room as a single person. They do it with ease and assurances they are quite accurate. Actually pisses me off sometimes."

"Yeah, me too, but we will. They see a part of all this we do not yet. They both talk often as though they have come here from a future so far away now is a mythology, as if they are speaking from remembrances."

"Theresa was talking to me one day, and I asked her how she knew this would come to pass, how could she be so sure that she would dedicate her life to things the rest of the planet shunned, feared, and struck out at. 'I have seen it' is all she said."

"How does she know she doesn't imagine it? I mean how do we know? Jesus, someone just tried to blow us up, someone held a gun to you, and in a few hours were walking into a time bomb of emotions directed at us like bullets. What the fuck are we doing?" Amanda said with tension in her voice.

Sarah turned still in her arms and pulled her close to her, just holding her until she felt the tremors subside deep within her. Healing is a hug sometimes, just a simple hug and knowing how long to hold on.

"Look, Sarah, I am not doubting anything. I just wonder sometimes if we are sane, even though I know we are, by a standard the rest of the world measures insanity by." They parted and laughed like junior high school girls, healing complete.

"Peter told me once, that imagination is easy to see working, you can observe yourself piecing it together, filling in the blanks, adding and subtracting the bits and pieces until it forms the picture you desire it to, a still life you need to animate. Vision forms its own picture and pushes into your mind like an intruder into your home. It doesn't ask your permission, it is just there regardless of your place or circumstance, nothing needs adding, it is all there, sight, sound, smell. Vision takes your senses and uses them as it needs to," Sarah said.

"Makes sense. Yes, it feels right. Like our empathic

perceptions, feeling great, then all of the sudden a dark emotion hits the solar plexus, shoots up to the pineal gland and across the bridge to the pituitary, chakras come to full alert."

"But the navigation through situations, this requires more than intuition, almost as if you're standing in the solution seeing how you 'did' get through it before you engage it. Theresa and Peter do that naturally, is if there is no other way known to them. Peter and I talked a lot of the abuses I suffered, and his also. The conversations were about the abilities those circumstances refined in us. We were always thinking ahead, using data from the previous to see the scenarios playing out in the mind. Damage couldn't be avoided, but it could be minimized. Intuition led me to study what I needed to, and circumstance forced its reality, like being able to project out of my body during molestation episodes, learning to stay in a meditative frequency as my natural state."

"I recall all our talks as children, late at night under the covers whispering, reading together out in the woods. My God, Sarah, we were never little kids, we were adults in little bodies. I sometimes cry for the little girl that never lived. But look at us now, so in love and so different than we could have ended up."

"I remember being little on the playground at school, feeling like an alien, none of the other kids talking to me or asking me to play. Kids sense the difference more than adults and they are just afraid of what they feel. Peter told me that most of his life he felt he was evil incarnate, hiding and controlling a great evil within himself, afraid to let it into the world. So much rage and anger."

"He seems so gentle now though, Theresa too. But there is an undercurrent of a power that could destroy worlds in them both. I feel it every time I am near Theresa."

"She would say 'that's your own shit, child' as is her way,

doesn't mince words much, does she? But that's what I love about her, she is right there in the open, fearless and powerful. She is the crone that people fear, but cannot avoid being drawn to. I guess we have much to learn."

"So, we need to go to church, eh? Think the roof will fall in? I haven't been to a church since I was little and my parents made me go to pray for my brother to be found. This should prove to be one of our more interesting encounters with the locals." Amanda was primping her hair as she talked, a nuance that depicted nervousness.

"Peter and Theresa have just entered the building, we should go and greet them."

"Yes, I want to stop by the child room and check on some kids, were close to this ring stealing kids and shipping them to the Middle East, it would seem there is a great demand amongst the rich and perversely sick to pay upwards of one million dollars for young Anglo kids. We need to network with more of us in that area of the world."

Sarah went into the bathroom to finish her hair. There was a "crack" sound in the other room, she peered out to see what it was, a small noise but unusual enough to look.

It is amazing how seconds can alter lives into even future generations. Some occurrences can cause DNA to shift its shape and pulses forever. Time stops to allow for the ripples that will emanate from the moment into life, choosing its own speed and its waves will never cease as it finds its way into a universe, stopping all others in its passing.

Sarah saw Amanda on the bed, sitting, her eyes staring right into Sarah's.

All looked as it had when she entered the bathroom, save for the little hole in Amanda's forehead and the lake of red behind her. Her eyes holding to life long enough to meet Sarah's eyes. She felt her enter her consciousness with rapid motion of her energy, it pushed Sarah back onto her heels to find balance. The very reverse of the coffee shop ability to transfer energy. This was far more than Amanda saying good bye to her lover, this was Amanda's essence entering her.

Sarah stayed locked to her eyes until they closed for the final time and she fell back on the bed. Sarah dropped to her knees and let out a scream that shook all presence outward and inward, until angel and human stopped to feel her anguish.

As Theresa and I entered the great room, the sound of Sarah's scream echoed throughout the room, until it was full. They looked at one another as hyper awareness filled them in on what was transpiring upstairs in the loft room. We each sprang to action in our own way. I was bounding for the stairs as Theresa followed screaming orders into a cell phone. We hit the door together, knowingness filled our awareness as we walked closer to the sight their minds were finding hard to process.

Sarah was on the floor as she had fallen, still gasping for air between screams. Amanda lay on her blood that had filled the bed now, she was dead.

"Go to Sarah," I commanded. "I am going upstairs to the bell tower, she is up there!"

"She who?" Theresa demanded.

"Our little FBI lady, Angie. She did this. Tend to Sarah," I said, walking towards the stairs.

I exited the last step as my eyes found my target, Angie standing near the rail looking over the edge, gun still in her hand, the other gently draped on the rail. Any other moment in time I would have seen her looking quite picturesque in this setting, even beautiful.

"Why?" I demanded.

"I missed, I was supposed to kill Sarah. Amanda is a casualty of war. I was still standing there when Sarah came out, but I could not shoot her, something inside overrode the programming and would not allow me to kill her, so I came up here."

"That's it? That is all you have to say?"

"What do you want to hear, Peter? I killed her and was sent here to do just that, and you knew it too when they were interviewing me. You just ignored that little something you couldn't put your finger on. She knew too, just not when, and she ignored it because she too wants to know why."

"Is there a why?" I asked.

"Of course there is a why. Money, selling children on a global market, billions. Sarah and her little dyke Amanda were about to uncover it, and that cannot happen!"

"And this is how you intended to hush it up, killing Amanda and Sarah? How the hell do you think this will work? What, you're going to kill all of us? Oh and don't forget to kill the two agents downstairs, and the couple of hundred other people that are involved with the program. Good plan!"

"You Americans are so smug, your arrogance clouds your judgment, we count on it and we have never been disappointed," she sneered.

"Americans? And you would be?"

"I was born in Denmark, but all of this is rather irrelevant at this stage, wouldn't you say? This is bigger than you can imagine, we are talking thousands of people in every country in the world. In answer to your question, killing everyone in this town would not be ruled out, these people kill anything in their way, anything—anyone. Shut them down and they are back online in an hour, kill them and others take their place immediately. I became an FBI agent for this very reason, to monitor them, they are beyond stupid."

"So, all of this, the explosion, the old woman, all of it was about this?"

"Of course it was. You think this is over? I will not go to prison and you will be lucky to survive the night, you and all your New Age cronies. New world? Are you serious? It is a joke and so is this place and all of them like it. This is the real world my friend. In the real world children are bought and sold like cattle, sold into slavery, sex rings, and let me clue you in on something, it has been this way since the first human threw their child into the fire to warm themselves on a winter night, and it will always be this way, even when we are living in the universe as this place foresees it, we will still be selling children for perversions, and the rich will pay as they always have, except we'll be doing it in a much larger market. Perversion, drugs, alcohol, these are the truest markets of the world, these are what feed the empires, and America is the most perverted of all."

"Well, that was a fine dissertation on the human condition. Remind me to write that down for later reference."

"You forget I am still holding a gun."

"No, I did not forget, it clashes starkly with your bracelet. You're fucking with the wrong New Ager honey. I am old school, before this new era. I know your kind, and yes, there are millions of you, like any virus, like plague carrying rats. I don't doubt anything you said, none of it. I also have a talent for seeing into the past and the future. I have seen vividly the humans that threw their children into fires, more than we will ever look at, and that is just one atrocity in countless ones across time. Spiritual people do in fact have a common trait of burying their heads in the sand and up their asses. Airy fairy magical incantations and ancient traditions of dying like sheep in the slaughter for God, country, and American pie. The New Age is a business, just like the ones you do, selling pipe dreams to desperate people and ones looking for 'alternative' magic pills to figure out their own lives. The age of the victim reaped the age of the New Age conglomerate. If I can't sell it on my own, I'll just channel it through Michael the Arch angel, who's going to argue with him?"

"SO, you're just like me then? How delicious."

"No sweets, I am nothing like you. In a few moments this tower will look like bees have swarmed it, all the heartfelt New Agers you're speaking of will go primal when they hear of this, and you'll be lucky to just end up dead. So here is what's going to happen. Out of unbelievable remorse for your actions, you're going to jump off this tower onto the hard concrete below, because it truly is your only choice for a quick exit out of this, and as painless as it's going to get for you. Are you getting this yet?"

"You're joking, I am standing here awaiting the arrival of people that will make primal seem welcomed. They will kill anyone without asking, human life means nothing to them, and they hardly fear your law enforcement. I am walking out of here, alive and well, you idiot."

"No, I guess you're not getting any this. Your people are not coming because we didn't miss it when we talked to you, we just acted as if we did. Let me tell you about what you think we don't know. The ring you think is such a powerful secret is well known and has been for a while. We also knew that you were going to kill Sarah, you jumped ahead on your own today, trying to show some incentive for your superior Neanderthals. Don't take it personally, we're just more evolved than you know. There are two to three thousand people involved in over seventy countries. Your superiors will kill you for this and you know it, because as we speak people are being arrested globally, kids are being rescued, and this really is the last day of your life, Angie."

"You're insane, you know that, all of you here are fucking insane. You live in this fantasy world that will come crashing down on you like hell rising."

"That makes no sense, but the mind does that when it is shorting out in the face of realities greater than itself. Your life is passing before you as we speak, are you remembering your life in sexual slavery after you were taken? I am truly sorry for that, but you made the choice to stay in the life you detested, now you're beyond willingness to even save yourself. You have played so long that there is no you anymore. After you grew to adulthood, you could have made other choices, instead you chose this. Welcome to your choices. While you were here you could have reached out and changed it all, killing Amanda was the point of no return, your subconscious desire to end this once and for all."

"You really believe all this New Age crap, don't you? You really believe that in 2012 a new world will actually appear and all will be splendid and joyous. That people can evolve by will, and all the 'healers' are actually making anything better. You're beyond saving, my friend, just as I am, you're just as dead in your reality. Is pandering The Secret to the poor and desperate any different than accommodating the world's perversion, both will be here long after we are gone, Peter, and you know it. Starchildren, Indigos, Stargate watchers, my God! Can you see any sanity in any of this? Everyone here walks around thinking they are some evolved race of new humans, telepathic communication? This has to end as much as what I do does, but it never will. Do you really believe that I had some sort of choice about leaving these people? I was abducted when I was seven years old and fucking forty-year-old Arabs a week later and for the rest of my life. I would still be in Belgium being passed around by oil Czars if I hadn't begged to take this cover in the FBI."

"You could have opened up when you got assigned in Cleveland."

"Now who doesn't get it. You're not that stupid, Peter. I would not have lived a day after talking. Security is illusion, safety is a lie, and justice is as much of a business as Exxon oil. The 'people' that stole me from my home are the same ones that run credit card companies, literally. Are people in debt able to get out before they die? No more than I was able to. True MasterCard won't kill you, they'll just make you homeless until you die thirty years early. Ten thousand murders a year go unsolved and hardly investigated in just this country, I dare you to count them worldwide. It's all show, Peter, all of it, with a very small fraction of the entire population controlling it all."

"All true, all of it, I know it, you know it, and every person that is swiping a credit card knows it. That is the price of apathy, not the result of powerful people exercising power. Those people run the world, not governments, companies or the infamous 'people' of democracy. One week of consumers taking a break from consuming would tip the scales forever, and they know that too, and we know that won't happen. People of the rain forest know that when democracy comes, they will need to pay for what they walk into the forest right now and get freely. But they will not stop it. All true. But what has this to do with the choice you need to make right now."

"I could just shoot you, obviously I am a very good shot."

"But you won't."

"You don't know that."

"Yes, I actually do. You would have done so when I entered. You couldn't kill Sarah and Amanda was just 'there' and your superiors would not notice if you didn't kill someone. But you won't kill me for the same reason that you couldn't Sarah, because through your training something occurred you never counted on. You developed your own powers of empathic abilities, you couldn't kill her because as long as there is a chance of truth here, you can not do it. You spent too much time in the child find room not to begin to open up and see the results they achieve, and you also saw the demise of your child slavery business there. You saw this moment. What will you do now?"

"Yes, Angie, what will you do now?" It was Theresa's voice at the doorway.

She crossed over to Angie in that floating way of hers, keeping her eyes locked to Angie's, fear was turning her whiter as Theresa moved closer, She came to rest an inch from the frightened woman's face.

"Yes, Angie, do tell us now, what will you do?"

She turned to me as if Angie was not there. "Sarah is on a plane along with Amanda's body, the center is locked down, all the children sent home, and there is an army of monks here to achieve the next step. All is going according to plan, except this little unforeseen timing of events." She returned to looking at Angie's eyes.

"It's time, my dear. There have been six arrests at the Cleveland FBI, and eight more left by way of the upper windows. The director is barricaded in his office, I suspect a single shot will be heard shortly, and the people you're awaiting have been diverted to Mexico. They are now talking to a policeman whose daughter was found in a Brazilian governor's basement, strapped to a wall. Some of your work we presume. You had to pull something off soon, because those you work for were impatient at how so many abductions you set up went wrong, children never arriving at pickup points. They also believe you're responsible for what is occurring in their world. The same is happening all over the globe, as it is a global sting. Any last words?"

"You fucking bitch, you're no different than those that stole me away. Look at all the death in your wake. You fucking hypocrites, America deserves to die. You preach love for children, bullshit. You drop them off to anybody that will watch them for you, you pervert them with everything you manufacture and sell, and the ones that keep them busy enough not to bother you sell the most. Daycare centers are pedophile heaven, like a shopping center for them. Seventy percent of the kids I have stolen come from daycare workers. You have no idea who you're fucking with."

"Neither do, you dear."

"You think your sting is going to stop anything? Those that run it probably organized it to clean out their own house. The police, FBI, CIA, they have no idea how used they are or by whom. I was sold for the week to senators, judges, congressmen in over seventy countries before I hit puberty. There has not been one society in history that cared a rat's ass about kids. Has all the popular shows in America stopped it? Even slowed it down? Did Oprah stop it, or just get rich off of it?"

"No, not anymore than killing Amanda will stop this, in fact you only moved it forward. I assure you with every atom of my being, this will never go unsensed again, no one will ever get past the radar in the world now, no one will ever get this close again to harm one of these children. We are more than you will ever live to see. Now—CHOOSE!"

In a flash, the gun came up under her chin, the trigger was pulled and the blast sent her over the edge to the pavement below. A wave of Theresa's hand from above brought a van to the body, it was scooped up and put into the van, seconds later the walk was being hosed down.

I looked at Theresa now for the first time since we found Amanda and Sarah. I looked deep into her eyes and reached for her, she fell into my arms, where we stayed until night fell.

XIV
Amazing, Just Amazing

When two empaths hug each other it is a profound feeling. There are no lies and no deceptions. One feels the subtle energy flowing deeply and they have a way of restoring the flow to one another's hearts. An empath can hug you with pure energy and envelope you in a way few can, even across long distances.

Sarah's grief was beyond description, yet we both knew to stay away from sensing her right now, she had to deal with this herself before anyone else could enter her space. Then there was this new development of Amanda's essence within her. This was something we needed to understand quickly and completely. This was a new step in the evolution of ability. So many questions to be answered.

The idea that everything was interconnected in creation comes to light in this event in a way only fiction writers dared imagine.

"We must get into gear here, Peter," Theresa said as she rose to her feet again. "There is time enough for grieving later."

"I can't believe what has happened here today. Sarah had told me the whole plan before I got here. It sounded simple enough, but plans are triggers that set things in motion, once done, it takes on a life and direction of its own power and emotion."

"So many variables in the equation, too many to see ahead of time, too many to walk through clearly sometimes. Angie was an empath herself, she would not have survived her life had she not been, so she knew that striking was a matter of shutting down all her emotions to walk unseen."

"Yes I know, I sensed her as a blank spot moving through the center, a true ghost. Where is the son of the woman that was blown up?"

"He is on his way to Cleveland with the two agents, we asked them to take him there, primarily to get them all out of here, and to let them do what they may with the man. He was Angie's contact for delivery of the kids she tried to abduct, a soulless bastard that was motivated by money. He knew his mother was going to die, but was being paid well for the set up. The little demonstration out front was the set up to make it appear a religious fanatic was behind the violence. Angie was seducing him to make him comply, and he was eating it up like it was real."

"There is still the matter of the churches involvement, how deep is it?"

"We know the pastor was the primary contact for Angie and those in Europe, the kids were being moved out through the churches youth camps, never abducted there, either on the way or leaving from a rest stop or store. The son would follow them, abduct them, and Angie would set up the drop of the child. We had intercepted most of the kids in the last few months. We created a diversion at the kidnap point making taking them impossible. We tried to keep it as natural as possible looking, a group of people from the center would just stay around the family making the kidnap too risky with so many witnesses."

"The pastor is going to be dangerous with these new events this evening."

"True, I am sure he has tried to make contact with his people in the federal building in Cleveland by now, and is aware they are all dead or in custody. I can feel his panic now. He is not a man that will face this, he will try to run."

"Where is Angie's body?"

"It is being taken to Cleveland for the FBI to deal with, fake or not, she was still theirs, let them deal with her. Two of the monks are transporting her. They are all from the Ashram in Cleveland, and we have close ties with them, they are here to protect us and to keep order, a contact we have in Cleveland, Francis, sent them. There are two of them downstairs waiting for us, they will be with us wherever we go now."

"I can feel them there, amazing energy control they are exhibiting. There is an actual energy barrier between them going across the doorway."

"Yes, they are highly evolved also, more so than the world has been allowed to witness. What they use to do with martial arts, they now do with thought. We are new to this world we live in, Peter, we are discovering wonders in human evolvement with each step we take, people that have silently evolved in their chosen crafts and arts, now coming into play in the light of day. Amazing things are occurring. With more amazing people coming into our awareness."

"Angie was also a highly evolved version of human ability, Theresa. She was able to cloak herself for a long time here. Had we not noticed the emptiness in her presence, we might not have discovered her at all. She was the new predator, and a lot of the kids being rounded up across the globe right now are going to have the same talents from their torture."

"True, but now we know them, we know how to sense them."

"We also know that exposing them causes an almost programmed self destruction sequence to begin. We must find a way to stop that before it begins. So many caught in Cleveland chose to dive out of windows, and they don't have windows that open, it took a lot of determination to break them."

"Most had families and were respected members of their own lives, shame is still a basic driving force in our culture. Those that had Angie's experiences are no strangers to shame and its emotions, they can override it easily, but those that just pretended to be wholesome people, it hits them like a bullet that encompasses their whole being. Some, like the director barricaded in his office, still seeking a clear path out, but when he sees there is none, he will choose the one Angie did."

"I knew when I saw her up here she had already decided. She wanted us to know that when a child is raised in that horror, there is no other possible conclusion to their life. Even the kids being rescued now will always be as her at some level."

"I felt no remorse as she raised that gun to her chin, and I felt the relief she did as she died, it was probably the only relief she felt in her entire life. I sensed no memory of her life before her abduction. She was a biological machine. Her manipulation of the old woman is classic religious programming being used to elicit an outcome the opposite of the persons professed core beliefs. It was perfected in the Catholic mass, a ceremony repeated weekly, one the observer does not understand fully. It is a subtle programming to be activated later. The person believes they believe in something, yet at the core is an open mind willing to do the will of the programmer, the priest. At the core, there is no belief at all, only a blind willingness to do what 'God' wants."

"I think she was correct about this being planned by those doing this. There was an announcement out of Belgium three days ago about impending prosecution and charges coming down. The elite have been far removed, and the announcement was a trigger to 'clean house' to all those below them."

"I know, the other centers snatched up most of the kids as they were being moved to new locations. We are awaiting word on how many 'Amandas' we lost in the last three days.

The announcement in Belgium was our cue to move also. One press conference sent tens of thousands of human beings into motion, synchronized by their own intents. The child center downstairs is the only thing active right now, the monks are assisting the others, were tracking the kids from there and getting reports about the other centers globally and their successes, or failures."

"What's next, Theresa?"

"We go to church as planned, and then we turn over the center here to others, and eventually we meet Sarah."

We walked down the stairs to the level of the girls' room. There were monks moving in and out of the room, some in traditional robes, some in suits, and some yet in just jeans and T-shirts. Only their bald heads and demeanor made us aware of their identity. The room had been stripped clean of everything, it was an empty room now. All the personal items were packed and ready for transport, and some people were washing the walls down and cleaning the carpets. It is clear of the horror of a few hours ago, but now we walked into the center of the room to clear the rest. As we entered we were engulfed in the emotions of the moment, the sadness and the rage, the shocking emotions of what people do to one another. We stood there absorbing like a sponge, transmuting it as it passed into us. When we felt the last of it pass into us and out again, Theresa asked the some of the monks to meditate in the room for a few days, then it would be truly clear.

Theresa and I walked into the great room, it had been restored fully as it had been before all of this. The monks were using it as a meditation center now, with at least ten of them in meditation around the clock. The sleepy little town now rocked in reality of the human condition did not realize the profound effect these simple monks were having on the entire town. Meditation by such people is as a flood into an area, the energy saturates everywhere and into everything. In a sign of the new times, there were Amish men and women sitting in the room also, praying with the same powerful energy of the monks. Somewhere in the atmosphere they joined and became power enough to bring peace to this place.

Theresa went to one of the monks and spoke with him, while another walked over to me and introduced himself after bowing to honor our spirits.

"I am Ron from the Cleveland Ashram. Were here to assist in this endeavor in any way we can. There are around fifty of us here give or take with all the coming and going."

"Peter," I said, returning his greeting. "I am sure your assistance is well appreciated. I know Theresa and Sarah are greatly appreciative."

"We are all so very sorry about the one called Amanda. We had met them both a few times when they came for talks about opening of the center in Cleveland. This is however a great time for us all, spiritual people joining together in such an project as ushering in these new times."

"Yes, it's been a real hoot so far. But I feel tonight will find the morning sun shining again," I said, as Theresa walked back over to me.

"We are going to leave for the church now, a driver is coming around front to get us, six monks will be accompanying us. The pastor is still there, I sense he is going to bolt after the service is over. One of the women that come here is a caregiver for his mother at his home, she said he packed this evening and his stuff is in his car. I have dispatched some people to disable his car, just in case he smells us coming. Whatever has happened, he and Angie were running this show for this part of the country, them and some people at the FBI out of Cleveland, and before the dawn comes, I am sure others in high up position will be arrested or dead in Cleveland. If they were not operatives, they were clients."

"Things like this are always an exercise in escalating involvement, they will turn on each other to keep out of jail and the papers, but I doubt many of them will. The wires will be lit far into the night, and far across the state. The tentacles of this will reach into the capitals and beyond," I said.

"Each center in each state has a night like this ahead of them. Let's get to the vehicle," she said, walking towards a side door.

We walked out the door and directly into a van waiting with six monks accompanying us, two in front and four others in the lead car. I believe they were assuring us privacy to talk in the arrangement of people. We got in and settled across from one another to talk.

This was all feeling like a movie I saw once, but did not care for because the drama was not comfortable, just when you thought things would settle, they would explode. Makes great ratings, but not so great living in real time.

Theresa pushed lightly against an ear piece connecting her to the Child room at the center.

Listening intently, I tried to read her, but she was not showing herself.

"Worldwide there are approximately four hundred children in protective custody now, six of our people have been killed and ten wounded, and law enforcement has at least fifty dead or wounded. In Iran they are killing the children, as well as in Malaysia, and in Syria. African countries have not reported in. There have been fifteen hundred arrests made, and suicides are not being measured until this is over. It will take months to round up clients off line. The day before this these porn sites were getting ten thousand hits a day at one hundred dollars a movie, five hundred for direct web cam. Child rape, sodomy and incestuous role-playing were the top sellers. Snuff films were running neck in neck with the child porn. Our dead are being shipped to their families' towns. They are accompanied by someone from each center to explain fully to the family what they were doing and why."

"This is almost unbelievable. Angie was correct, the world still operates this way and regardless of what we become, there will always be this in our midst, it will run when humanity breaks out into living in space, but it will breed wherever it can."

"True enough, Peter, but it will be on the run from now until time runs out. Eventually they will self extinct, as in the suicides we are witnessing now, but it will be long after we are a mist in the cosmos."

"My God, Theresa, how did it get this far tonight? Body counts, wounded, Amanda dead, and on a global vastness."

"When you're exploring and lift a stone to find a viper's nest beneath it, you just exposed creatures that will bite and kill for having invaded their secret nesting place. Angie was testament to that reality. The viper doesn't wait for you to announce your intention, it just kills you then surmises your intent. When we were looking for missing kids, we happened upon a pattern in the abductions, revealing eventually a nest of vipers. Many nests all connected to one nest, but the mother nest was a web with many strands in many countries. Our psychics picked up on the vastness of it, it took months to begin to get a picture of its size. The two agents you met tried to do something through channels but were dismayed at the lack of interest they had to the information being given to headquarters, and the evidence being dismissed as too sketchy. Now we know why."

"Transition in human affairs is always tense business, but this is a scale I never imagined. But then these are times of transition humanity has plodded along for centuries talking of but refusing to comprehend it's full impact. I know that in a week, those sites will up and running again and the child train into this shit will be operating fully, with new engineers and new vipers in place. I suppose it will have to be enough to know some got away, some will be home tomorrow and repairing their lives."

"For now, yes. The real changes are happening at this level, small towns, new centers teaching real time ideas about new parenting, staying in contact with their kids in new ways. Empaths are evolving as the majority of the world population now. In our time, yours and mine, we were the different ones. Now we are apart of the majority, but so many walk about not knowing it. It is turmoil in their minds, struggles in their lives, and pain they cannot identify. The network of centers operating tonight are warriors with powers that a generation ago was science fiction. Just as these monks, they can stop you from breathing with a thought, but they would not ever think such a thought, some things must evolve naturally, and extinguishing a life for the sake of righteousness is not the natural order."

"It would have been nice to know this when we were young, but not knowing drove me to learn veraciously and evolve to escape my own circumstances. A shorter version of what I am sure Angie's life was, and Sarah's. Amazing, to similar lives, with two completely opposite outcomes."

"Angie was as the hostage in captivity so long that she forgot there was any other life to live. She became her captor's ideals to survive. Death was sweet relief. When this is over and Sarah is back, there is to be a conclave in Cleveland from the centers directors from all over the world. Just like the old days, a gathering of the wise. Who would have thought Ohio would be a place of such an event. Yet I saw this years ago, as you did also, Peter, or you would not still live here. Nor would I. When I separated from my husband, I wanted to leave here so badly, but then Sarah wandered into my life. The rest is unfolding in this van."

"We are walking in the unknown. At some point we ask, who are we, really? The question catapults us into reality beyond our names, places, and solid ground, into the essence of the mist that was us at one time. No cities, no states, no countries, no labels, and no identifying markers for us to grab, just 'you' looking back to see that the purposes our lives became were the ones we chose along the way. God did not appear to us in a burning bush and say this was our mission, we had no purpose until we stood in God place and gave ourselves one."

"Tonight is one of those times, there is only emotion to walk on, feelings creating the path, and it is all ignoring the dynamics of physics and the laws of reality. No one has an identity in this tonight, just a revelation of purpose and intent. In this there are no borders or countries, only a web of human interaction, good guys and the bad guys, with our people slipping in before and after because we don't have the privilege of waiting to see who is who. We are the empaths, the meek that are now inheriting the Earth."

"We're almost there," the driver piped in.

Theresa closed her eyes, and I followed her example. A moment to recharge, to recenter, and touch the pure. Before I closed my eyes, I noticed the driver had also closed his eyes, amazing, just amazing.

XV
Salvation

We arrived at the church, and took a few more silent moments before exiting the vehicle. It was a large church of typical American Christian style, all white with a steeple and a plain white cross on top. The parking lot was very crowded, and we were parked right in front of the church. A man was heading out of the doors to tell us we could not park there I am sure, then retreated back into the doors hastily upon seeing six monks in traditional robes emerge from our vehicles.

I am sure this was done deliberately for effect, I liked it, a lot.

Theresa smiled for the first time that evening seeing the man run back into the church to sound the alert. The monks formed a three and three wedge for us to be enveloped in, and we wasted no time, moving swiftly into the doors. We entered a large lobby, obviously large enough for congregating after services. There were three sets of doors entering the main church, with only the center ones being open. We headed for them like a large giant red bird, with robes flowing in our passage.

We entered the main aisle of the church, while in the side aisles TV cameras were focusing on the pulpit and the target of our interest. We had apparently interrupted a sermon.

"Smile wide, Peter, we're on TV," Theresa whispered to me.

The monks moved into flanking position on either side of us, anticipating us walking up the long aisle. But we just stood there a moment surveying the land, while a sea of heads turned their necks to see what had just invaded God's home.

The TV cameras swung to our direction and the pastor waved frantically to tell them "NO" but they were not listening.

The pastor was frail looking up there, with a look of fear a child could read. He was in his late fifties, perhaps early sixties, balding, with a round almost childlike face. A bit portly one would say, but his white suit was the icing on the evangelical cake. Pastor Robert Burke, a fixture in this community for decades, the man behind the power base of money and old wealth, born and raised here, and one hell of a model American, to be sure.

"Shall we kick ass and take some names, my dear?" I asked.

"Indeed, let's," she replied coyly.

"Good evening, Pastor Burke, how are you this fine evening?" she bellowed from the back.

"Well this is highly unusual I must say. What can we do for you this evening, and your uh 'friends' in the brightly colored robes. You are interrupting my sermon here, after all," he retorted.

"Well, Pastor, I understand you're taking a trip after this service, and I desired to speak with you before you left."

We were all walking very slowly as the dialogue unfolded up the center, with the monks keeping perfect rhythm with us, we had all adopted Theresa's floating style it appeared. Watching the people watching us was eerie feeling, as if they were watching the first encounter with aliens.

"Tell me, Pastor Burke, where are you going?" she asked with an obvious force in her voice.

"I know you, woman, you're Theresa, the new mayor's ex wife. You work at that spiritual center of the devil. Where a faithful woman of God was blown to pieces and her son was accosted. I hear tell there was a shooting there this evening too."

"You hear tell do you? I see the esteemed ex mayor is in the front row with his wife next to your own. The gangs all here as they say. I would have preferred to do this in private, but your escape makes it necessary to do this here and now. It has been quite an eventful day sir, eventful indeed. Let me correct some of what you said though. First, she was a religious fanatic, not a faithful woman of God, and her son abducted children, for you. Yes, there was a shooting at the center tonight, and a beautiful young woman died, her name was Amanda."

"She was a lesbian, lovers with that other harlot Sarah, abominations to God, both of them. She deserved to die in the eyes of God, and rot in hell," he mocked.

"Careful there, Pastor, you're already on broken ice. She was shot by a business partner of yours, Angie, the FBI agent you stole children with and sold them on the global sex market, from your own youth camps, by your sainted woman's son."

The place became verbal bedlam, with people jumping up in their pews and yelling, waving their fists, and children were being taken out of the main room, but the TV cameras kept on rolling. The monks began to encircle us, we had made our way up to the pulpit, a few feet away from the pastor. He began to wave his hands in a gesture to get everyone to calm down and sit back down. It took a few moments, but people finally returned to their seats.

The monks loosened their circle and fanned out in front of the pulpit to form a protective line and to observe, there was an obvious fear of these robed strangers.

"How dare you come in here, the house of God and tell such lies. HOW DARE YOU! I have been pastor to this church and town for twenty years, I love everyone here, especially the children. You have made this a house of the devil with your presence, I demand you leave here now!" He was screaming by this point, his face as red as the robes before him.

"We are not going anywhere until this is finished." Her voice was steeled in their words, exuding a force even the congregation pushed back in their pews to avoid.

"We will stay her until Jesus returns if need be, Pastor Burke. I lost a beautiful dear friend tonight because of you. Have you called your friends in Cleveland yet? They won't answer, they're either in a jail cell now, or dead. Do you really believe you're just going to walk away from all of this? No chance, none in hell, none."

"You cannot prove anything you are saying, I am innocent, and you're just trying to destroy me as you have this town. We had a great life here until you opened that place, and who are these men, your hired killers?"

"They are monks, true men of God, they live what they preach, not use it as a cover for their perversions and control, as you and others sitting here have for so long. Before we opened that place, this town was dying, being sucked dry by you and your friends, it would have been a ghost town in ten more years, even with the university here." She turned now to the congregation. "You all know I speak the truth, all of you, I have seen many of your faces at the center, talked with you on your farms, and worked together to improve life. The programs we started work for you, you're making profits now, your children have stopped disappearing. For God's sake, open your hearts and minds. This man has been stealing your children from you, in this county and four others in his youth camps and daycare centers."

"I will not stand here and listen anymore to this, and TURN THOSE DAMNED CAMERAS OFF!"

The police chief stood up and walked slowly towards Theresa, as the monks closed ranks around her at his approach. He was wearing a suit and was wondering if leaving his gun at home may have been a mistake. He was known as an honest man though, he knew of a lot of the corruption, but also knew he was a small town police chief and vastly outnumbered and out financed.

"I know you, Theresa, you're an honest woman, but you

better be able to prove what you are saying here, or there will some serious slander charges being brought against you. The center has strange goings-on in it, to be sure. There was a shooting? Where are the bodies, Theresa? Where is the woman FBI agent? You're not above the law there," he said, watching the monks intensely as he spoke.

"Your FBI agent is on her way back to Cleveland, she shot herself. Call Cleveland and verify her arrival, they will be there in about twenty more minutes, but they may not answer, things are quite in disarray there as well," she said, looking back to the pastor.

"I will do just that when I leave. Now, what about this girl Amanda, who shot her?"

"The agent shot her, and her body is in a plane on her way to an undisclosed location, along with Sarah. That is all you will ever know about it I am afraid," she said.

"Ever hear of obstruction of justice, Theresa?"

"Yes, I have, and I have spent my whole life here watching it occur under your nose. Let's not play verbal chess here, all right? Let it go, Charlie, just let it go. Explaining children disappearing and ending up halfway around the world under your nose will keep you busy enough. Your move."

"Arrest her, Charlie!" the pastor was demanding.

"No he won't, because he is an honest man, and I think the truth interests him more right now. I am not here to debate with you, the truth is the truth, and it is that you, and others sitting here have been profiting by selling kids into sex rings, and it is your judgment day, Mr. Burke."

"Oh? So now you do the judging for God also?"

"I've got this one, Theresa," I said. "No, Mr. Burke, she does not, this judgment is your own doing, the result of your own actions and deceits. A beautiful girl is dead, and many others have lived a life of horror since they were little, you redefine the term perversion to an indefinable state and expression."

"And who might you be?" he inquired.

"God."

That was more than the man could tolerate within the confinement of his beliefs. He bounded over the pulpit directly at me. I swerved with his dive, catching him by the throat as he came down. When he landed he was on his knees. I lifted him by his throat with two fingers on each side of his windpipe.

"Interesting sensation, isn't it, Mr. Burke? Don't talk anymore, it just makes it worse," I said.

I noticed two of the monks smiling in recognition of technique. Some of the congregation were standing again, and the police chief had his cell phone in hand wondering if he needed to speed dial the office. But this was going to play itself to a conclusion regardless if the marines showed up.

"Listen, Mr. Burke, listen to what this woman is telling you. This has been a day of death and dying for a lot of people, your friends, your associates, your conspirators. She is trying to prevent anymore pain and suffering in this day. There is no one left to call, there is nowhere you can run, and nothing you can say or do to make this all go away. This is your day of reckoning, by your choices, by your hands. Jesus cannot help you, nor would he want to I suspect considering what you're hiding."

I released my grip on his throat. He adjusted himself in his suit, and then tried to run. This time the sheriff stopped him, knocking him to the floor and putting his foot on his back.

The TV crew was eating this alive, they had already called the station to expand coverage, it was now being picked up by national networking.

As if on cue, the doors burst open and the place was swarmed with men in suits, they fanned out all across the churches walls and blocked the doors to keep anyone from leaving. These were obviously agents, the center doors remained vacant with obvious activity happening outside. All eyes once again went to the center doors. The police chief was raising the pastor to a standing position as things once again were frozen in the limbo of anticipation.

Two of the agents walked to the front of the church and asked people to empty the front pew, while several more took charge of the pastor, and his wife, the ex mayor and his wife. Several more were scanning the people with pictures to match to faces, six more people were pulled aside out of the congregation. They were herded aside and surrounded by men that were obviously intent on keeping them that way.

A tall man ominous man entered through the center doors, followed by a equally tall and Hispanic-looking woman. They walked directly to Theresa and I, while the man kept intense watch on the surroundings, and the monks that had now encircled us once again.

"You must be Theresa. Of course you are Peter? I am Maria Dogliotti, European Interpol, special task force, and this is agent Saunders, CIA. All these other gentlemen are FBI special task force out of Washington, D.C. I assure you we are the 'good guys' as you have met some agents that were not so good. We shall talk, but now we have some warrants to serve to those people over there, so excuse a moment, please."

The woman walked over to the encircled group segregated earlier. She sat her briefcase on a pew and pulled out a stack of warrants and began serving them. Names were being called, rights were being read, and handcuffs applied. As each was served an cuffed, they were being led out the door to waiting vans. The whole process took less than fifteen minutes.

The place seemed to take an energy of freshness as they were taken away, feeling a heaviness lifted from the air. I was scanning the faces in the congregation, every emotion humanly possible was visible, from relief to fear, but one thing was certain, this evening would be forever remembered for generations to come.

Maria returned to us along with the CIA man, whose expression had not changed since his arrival. The mystique of the agency training, leaving one wondering if they were not actually cloning these people in area 51.

"Well, that takes care of that, as they say. We have returned eighteen children with us tonight, they are at the hospital, only because we want to use it as a reuniting area for them and the families. There are psychologists available. Some of the abducted children are now much older and seriously damaged. The reunions may not be as the parents pictured them. How are you doing? I am aware of the murder and suicide here this evening, and the explosion earlier on."

"We are doing well, thank you," Theresa said. "We were about to expose the good reverend when you came in. Quite an entrance I might add. Are you aware the whole thing was being televised?" she added.

"We cut them off from outside before we came in. Actually we have been here for a while. At least long enough to see your entrance. Quite an entrance yourself. The monks are an interesting touch. I am sure it was for a paralyzing effect. People are easily stopped with anything new in their otherwise mundane worlds."

"I assume you know of happenings in Cleveland as well?"

"Yes, it is why these agents are out of D.C., and not local. This is probably one of the largest operations since Iraq. It will be days before we can get an accurate assessment of the final outcome. I understand you lost six people in your 'organization' shall we call it. I am sorry for that, truly."

"Our organization is just a network of spiritual centers connected by the Internet. We share a common intent, like this evening's purpose."

"Please, let's not go there, were both intelligent women here. Your people have been there at every turn in this, showing up before, taking children out, and to supply information that even the CIA wasn't able to get. We asked their assistance to cover our butts in hostile countries, some of the countries were killing the children so they could not reveal anything."

"Yes, we heard that also. We all lost people we care for and that were of sincere hearts. Tell me, Maria, does this gentleman speak at all? He seems to be very interested in our entourage. Perhaps he would like to speak to these dear monks."

"Yes I would actually," he said, breaking his silence. "But I want more to talk to you and your friend there. I don't care what you say, there is a lot more to this than just some spiritual centers exchanging ideals on the Internet. You possessed information that was highly sensitive in countries we can barely operate in even with local agents indigenous to the regions, and I am not leaving until I know how and why. Is that clear?"

"My—my, you are straight to the point when you do speak, I can admire that. Is this where I get intimidated and quake for fear of my life and freedom?"

"You'll find it wise not to fuck with me, lady," he barked back to her.

"Really, you are in a church, please, language. I don't think we have anything to discuss here, I believe we are done talking. I liked it better when you were the strong silent type."

"You're playing a game you cannot win, I am with the CIA, not some local yahoo sheriff's department. I will have answers before I leave here."

I decided to chime in at this point. "I believe the lady said she was done talking to you. Ah, you're going to try and speak with intimidation again, don't, do not speak at all, just listen. You're here because your psychics, sorry 'profilers' alerted you to the fact they could not penetrate the activity they sensed here and other places globally. You're not here to fact find, you're here to recruit. The monks you're trying to read so intently are amongst the new breed also, which is why you can't read them, you need to expand beyond your current levels of perception to find them. Allow them to demonstrate, so you have something to report."

The man's expression went to shock, his face paling by the second, mouth gaping and hands grasping his chest, he flopped into the pew behind him, staring at me as if I was Satan incarnate. It took a few seconds to achieve this result. He was released as quickly, regained his composure, stood and walked to the door as briskly as his dignity would allow, out into the night. A few seconds later his car could be heard screeching into history.

"Point made," Maria said, looking at me intently. "Look, I know we are all embarking on a new reality in this world. Tonight, I have seen how new, and realize my folly is in believing it is a future event. I have a personal friend in Belgium that is a powerful psychic. I use her talents on many of my cases, this one especially, she has proven more effective than all of our technology. She told me of this new hybrid in spiritual realities, empath is what she calls you. How am I doing so far?"

"You are doing magnificently," Theresa said. "But it is not as mysterious as all that, Maria. It is humans doing what humans do, evolving, we have just somehow managed to eliminate the birth—death requirement for it to occur. It is a matter of choice and education now, powered by the great intellect of intuitively stored knowledge within the cells of very person on the planet. Evolution by choice and free will."

"I have read much on this subject, yet find myself unable to cross the bridge to belief in it. Although tonight may find me feeling differently in the morning. Where is Sarah Theresa? That man was to leave with her, not just information."

"We knew that. It is why he was given such a dramatic demonstration, and why Sarah was put on a private plane with Amanda's body. I cannot tell you where she is."

"I suspected as much," She continued. "Agent Saunders will not let this go, you know that. He was shaken to the core by what you did. When he recovers his senses, he will come at you until he finds her."

"What does he expect to find?" I asked.

"He doesn't know, and that's what the CIA likes most, unknowns that they may be able to be incorporated into their own agendas. The Marines were once the government's private army, now it is the CIA. Your government is a very scary entity in the global arena. The world remembers one profound thing about America, many countries have nuclear weapons, America is the only one to actually use them. They were first to employ psychics as far back as the 1940s as well. In short, there is no ability of technology or human potential that America has not been able to fashion into a weapon of some sort."

"Well that was refreshingly poignant," I said.

"Peter, truth is truth, and the rest of the world has waited long for America to grow up, realizing fully she is a young country, but she has become somewhat of a bully under recent administrations. Terrorism is hurting many countries, and America the least, yet she fuels most of the reasoning terrorists kill under. Many things she is accused of, she is guilty of. What has this to do with you, me, or some young woman named Sarah? Hope, hope that what comes from this country will change and bring to the world a larger heart than she has exhibited recently. That what seems to be happening in your network of 'spiritual centers' will be strong enough to raise ideals from here that once gave the entire world hope. I feel I have made powerful friends here tonight, but that man that just left is a powerful enemy you have made in this same evening."

Theresa rose, taking the woman's hand to lift her to her and embraced her fully. Maria returned her embrace, and I could sense great emotion rolling off them both for this evening drawing to a close, purposes coming to fruition, and exhaustion being recognized.

Regardless of an organizations size, a country's might, or a military's ability, it still comes down to people, what humans say and do in simple exchanges such as this one. A conversation is small town church can set historic changes in motion without the participants even desiring it or focusing on such lofty goals. A young woman liberating herself n a coffee shop can be later known as a declaration from the universe of a new epoch in human evolution and expansion of human beings into their rightful place of powerful life forms in a universe filled with uncountable lives.

"When I see Sara, I will tell her of you and this evening, and we will sit and talk again, Maria. Sarah is one of millions now walking Earth. Connected in ways science-fiction writers talked of, but reality presses ever forward regardless of our opinions and desires. Empath is a catchall word when no word can really apply or explain, but it is one for the present I guess. Sarah lost a dear lover and friend this evening, a childhood twin. But she will realize it is a loss we all will feel soon, losing what was to what is, with the same sadness. In a loss she also received a gainful leap into something totally new to us all and one we do not understand yet, but it mimics what the world is experiencing at present, the old falling away to something so new it will push history into the realm of irrelevance at is arrival."

"Well, at least tonight we made a difference in the lives of some children. I will have to be glad for that, and I am. When Sarah resurfaces I will want to talk with her. An FBI agent is dead, and good or bad, there has to be some closure for the records. The Cleveland office is a mess, and accountability of things will go on for months," Maria said.

"Actually, Maria, it was Theresa and I that were there when Angie killed herself. As we have explained, the body was taken to Cleveland for disposition. There are no reports on any of it, and there won't be. People will just have to get over it I suppose. The gun she used was transported with her, and the autopsy will validate the suicide. It is done."

"That is for you and locals to deal with, I intend to be back in Belgium by tomorrow evening. I am taking a vacation when this is done and filed into history. I am also leaving my contact information with you both, I would like it if you would keep in touch. I think that somewhere in near future our lives may be of service to things we are not seeing yet."

"I would like that very much, and yes, the future has many plans. Interpol and our little group seems an interesting blend of energies," Theresa said warmly.

Maria left and went to the hospital to oversee reunions with family. The church was all but empty now, with few stragglers hanging out and talking amongst themselves. Phone lines, and emails would be lit far into the night about all the news from this little corner of nowhere.

Maria seemed a genuine person, but a member of Interpol and very much a "cop" but with a smarter demeanor than her CIA counterpart. Both were focused on the unknown called Sarah. They seem to have had an impression she was a key to a new design of human being cloned from spiritual genetics. Correct, but not accurate. I reminded myself to ask Theresa to check on "missing" people from the global network.

Theresa was over talking to our monk friends, sending them on their way it seemed, for a good nights sleep, whatever they wanted to do. Protection was not what we needed right now, I do not think. Things were slowing down and it was time to face the reality that Sarah was out there, and Amanda was not anymore. I watched Theresa as she spoke to our friends, she was a striking woman with a dynamic energy, but tiredness was beginning to show, she needed rest. Like everyone in these times, communication and information are a part of your life like blood coursing through your veins. Real time dialogue, sensory input, and telepathic perception to be dealt with. It becomes a Zen exercise, yet one that speaks to you of life in the future, for our children and their great grandkids.

The human race was preparing itself for populating the universe within the disguise of its seemingly self destruction. Navigation through untold galaxies will require abilities of perception far advanced to even what we witnessed today. Regardless of our plans and ideas of ourselves, something operating subtly within ourselves is constantly creating a person far beyond our imagination, while at a deeper level, a connected consciousness is creating a race that can evolve into any dimension and find its balance and be fully human.

"Let's get out of here," Theresa said. "I am tired and oddly hungry. I sent the monks back to the center to rest and eat. They are going to the child find room to get updates, and I asked them to copy Maria on whatever we find, including the movements of our own. I think she can be trusted and I sense deep sincerity in wanting to move with all of this."

"Yes, I sensed it too, but the CIA guy is going to be a pain in the ass. He was reeking of determination of self promotion, a real 'one man army' attitude. He sped off, but he didn't leave, count on it. He is off somewhere searching his data banks for some explanation for what happened to him. During Viet Nam there were rumors of psychic assassins being used by the CIA, rumors, but I know some of the people they tried to train for it. The premise being the mind cannot tell real action from thoughts of the same action, imagine you went in and killed them, the end result should be a dead enemy. This guy wants Sarah because they believe she filling the missing blanks for the program."

"Then they must know about the coffee shop incident, and feel it to be a conscious act of assassination. They think empaths are going to dominate the world by this technique. How cute is that?"

"Yes, deadly cute. If they get her they will threaten her with jail in a federal prison for the murder of the old man. They can hold a person for, let's see, forever. If they get her she will never be seen again, nor will we. Ignorance always perceives the unknown as hostile."

"True, but back to center here, we are seeking ways of flowing into this, not fighting our way into it. As tonight went well, a lot of things that could have gotten even uglier went smoothly enough. This church could have ended up a battle sight, but instead it was a flow of energies one into another without major incident."

"It, we, all of us globally are out in the open now. The plan within the plan. Those that desired to live in the shadows for decades more will learn in the morning papers and news that there is no more shadow. I have seen on the Internet for years 'the veil is lifted' and now even those that wrote it will understand what that truly means. It was never a veil separating the cosmos from us, but one that shaded us all in ourselves. We're naked now, the Emperor's new clothes."

"Hell has been unleashed, the demons are angels chasing us all into our own fruition, we evolve now, or die. Let's walk back, Peter. I need to feel the air against my face, to see the stars, and hear the crickets right now."

"Sounds like a plan."

XVI
The Desert Keeps Her Secrets

The plane hit the ground about midnight, Israeli time. The Lear jet was being towed into a private hangar with seven passengers aboard. No border checks, nothing, a straight flight into the Israeli desert, a lone house out in the middle of nothing as it was intended to be.

The jet was the private one of a man that had supported Sarah's research and work since college, a connection of Theresa and her husband. A quiet billionaire that supported this endeavor with wealth and powerful friends.

Networking opens new avenues of secret things evolving in the world under the cover of the darkness of an overpowering and loud media circus. It is never what is in the news that matters, only the things happening outside of its radar. The news media is so controlled it believes itself to operate in total freedom of information, because that's what the controlling hands tell it.

Journalists in recent decades are the grown children that once snuck around playgrounds mentally collecting information they thought would create a drama once revealed, getting others into trouble to divert attention away from their own desire for chaos. Only to discover that most of the time, no one gave a damn what they had to say, and it changed little to nothing.

The people in the plane accompanying Sarah and her lover's body had seen the broadcast from the church, having counted on the veracious appetite of the media for anything that even promises to be human suffering. It would set them on a hunt for this new evolvement in human genetics, and as always, they would be directed into avenues they would think were of their own choosing.

Sarah sat motionless, as she had for almost all of the flight, deep in a trance only she knew the parameters of. Two of the strongest healers from the center had been monitoring her energy patterns since that fateful moment. Amanda's body lay in the back of the plane as if sleeping. People from the center had prepared the body before leaving according to ancient rituals only known by those that did it, but Theresa had given them the direction.

The plane was divided into two internal sections, the front holding the party traveling with Sarah, and the rear with Sarah and Amanda riding as alone as possible. Only Elaine and Francis had ventured into the rear compartment during the flight. They were well known energy workers throughout all the networks groups, often being asked to drop their lives and fly off to another country to assist in some manner.

Elaine had been born a healer, with a natural affinity for reading energy and aligning it without the person needing to be aware of it. She was originally Christian, being dragged from tent to tent by her father to heal the sick, for heavy donations. She was now in her forties with a kind of untidy look, hair combed, but not her priority ever. She always wore long dresses, usually dragging on the ground due to her short stature, but when she appeared, she dominated the atmosphere. She was very dark-eyed, with long black hair, against her pale skin, she gave the look of one possessed with a power that warranted stepping back and letting walk where it may.

Elaine was conferring with Francis in front of the rear compartment door. He stood there motionless, listening. The product of decades of self training, he was well known for his knowledge, specializing in aiding people to access their intuitive knowledge base.

He had studied almost every form of religion and spiritual arts, yet never joined any, he taught joining a particular belief instantly began to confine ones growth within that belief and its defining borders, borders and the new life forming could not ever be reconciled in his mind. He had lived at the Ashram of the visiting monks before coming to the center.

He had called them when things went down. He had blue eyes that pierced the Soul of the one they were on, making a statement somewhere in them that he would not waste their time, so do not waste his. Theresa chose him for this quality to accompany Sarah.

This was the ideal of this new transition, people that had once, not so long ago, been alone in their endeavors and pursuits, perfecting their idea of spiritual advancement and evolution, but seemingly awaiting patiently, this time of unified motion. In the early stages of such a monumental step forward the participants are equally in awe of their abilities. Like children finding their balance to walk, most now were learning to walk also, into new dimension of application of their once theories of human capability. Yet, as children, the fear of walking too often kept them crawling. Circumstances had picked them up and dropped them back to their feet with a definite command to "walk" or live forever on your knees.

A few years ago most of these people were in school, changing diapers, working ordinary jobs and living quite ordinary lives. They all had interest in spiritual practices, belonged to some local group, or played online with the groups that desired to make magic in their lives. But now they were into a life they only thought of in the place between awake and asleep, in silent meditations they thought would not crash into their real time lives.

Yet here they are, in the middle of a desert in Israel, accompanying a young woman that was seemingly in the midst of a transition few would ever understand, and many would fear. But one that the universe had somehow commanded the human experience to add to its DNA strand, a quickening not yet defined.

"We need to call Theresa," Elaine stated. "She is aware we

are here, but she wants details of the energy changes in Sarah's field, and they are great. I cannot enter that cabin without it feeling like I walked into a ice storm. I also have no clue as to what to do with this, do you?"

"No, I don't," said Francis, "but my sense says not to do anything at all, this needs to run its course within her, and she knows best what to do with it. On this trip we are observers only. We need to get off this damned plane, she needs the openness of the desert right now. Which is why we are here. Her energies are like a fire trying to reach outward and it is too confined in here."

"I would agree with that, go tell the others were leaving. I will go help her."

Francis walked back to the front compartment, and leaned over to the ear of the monk sitting in the first seat. He got up and began to open the door to the craft. The top and bottom of the door opening like a giant yawning mouth to let us out. The heat from the desert filled the cabin, feeling quite relaxing somehow to us all. The monk and the three others exited. Elaine was always accompanied by her latest students, usually two, while Francis remained his loner self in all circumstances. In a few seconds, the plane was empty save for Elaine, Francis, and Sarah. Elaine was sitting in a seat outside the rear cabin talking on a cell phone when Sarah appeared in the doorway.

Her energy appeared before she did, emanating through the door like flames purifying her way. At the center of her self was the motion of a raging storm, with dark reds, crimsons and deep yellows, an inferno of swirling energy, and as it flew into the air it culminated in icy white and blues, shooting from her essence like ice particles raining in all directions.

It was difficult to keep centered in the presence of this phenomenon, as fear tried to creep into the equation of what to do in its presence.

As she stood perched in the doorway, her eyes betrayed

nothing of what was transpiring in her depths, just an icy stare of someone so internalized one had to ponder if return was even possible. Her green eyes were large and intent on their inward gaze, as if an outward glance would allow a release of energy that would devastate all in its path.

Neither Francis or Elaine had ever witnessed such an intense emission of energy from a single human being. Francis could not take his eyes off the display, and noticed his own senses going into extreme filtration of the display, allowing it in to his sensory awareness a very little at a time, feeling too much would overload even his refined ability. Her energies appeared to be a cloak all about her, with only her face seemingly made of flesh anymore.

Sarah passed the two as if not seeing them at any level of perception and walked out the door and down the steps of the aircraft. The monk and others were at the bottom, all moved away as she floated past them, the monk using his arm to push the others back away from her passing. She stopped and turned to the doorway, where Francis and Elaine stood.

"Please bring Amanda's body. I am going into the open desert and I would like not to be disturbed, please do not follow me. I will return when I am ready. We will tend to Amanda's body when I return. I am fine, and I thank you for all you have done this evening."

She turned and walked in to the darkness. She illuminated it as she moved, like a "light upon the hill" from an old prophecy within a forgotten scripture. Colors swirled around her with changes unable to record in their speed and description. Her request was the first she had spoken since being whisked out of the centers room. Time had ceased in that moment, and had returned as of yet. The long flights hours were recorded nowhere except in the pilots mind and log books. Outside of that requirement, time itself no longer seemed relevant to anything anymore.

Three men from the house were tending to the body under

the monks direction, moving it into the home's cellar for cooling and preservation. Sarah had stood with it for the first hours of the flight, talking to her and murmuring over it. Elaine had witnessed her kiss Amanda, first on her forehead, then both eyes, finally on her lifeless mouth. She gently closed the lid of the box holding her dearest friend and lover, and she did not look at it again.

After Sarah's light could no longer be seen, all retired to the dwelling. Elaine and Francis were quite concerned leaving the girl to wander in an open desert at night, but knew her well enough to let it go. But Elaine did call Theresa immediately.

So much was occurring, so many people in motion, so many places, and this, this new development that Elaine could be allowing to walk into history. But such circumstance are where human beings become the most ingenuous, clever, and inventive. Here all must be left to trust and that arena humans are most apprehensive of, no control. Tonight each person playing a part must come to terms with themselves as an evolving piece of the whole, or a rugged individualist falling into a voluntary extinction. There must be trust that each will know what to do within their own arena of action, to think as individuals that are a part of the whole, realizing with each choice, the whole will be affected with the same impact as the individual. Yet, this new dimension we have breeched is human friendly and sensory sensitive as well. It gives substance to the reach for trust on such a massive scale, seeing individuals moving with precision, and whole companies of people as one, there was a flow that was a goal all too often, and never a realization.

Elaine and Francis finally resigned themselves to go into the home of this generous man, one that sent a private jet halfway around the world to pick a young woman he barely knew, yet had hoped for all his life.

The house seemed odd for that of a billionaire, a little dwelling, almost as one would see in a typical suburb. Yet things in these times are never what they appear, and this was a lesson that needed to become second nature to all participants. Even the hangar that housed the Lear jet looked like a typical pole barn.

Francis assessed the situation quickly, this was all for show, a simple house that could be searched quickly and without result, and a simple outbuilding. This was a citadel that looked to be nothing opposing governments would look at twice, regardless of who claimed ruling power in the area.

His mind flashed backwards as it often did, as memories in his cellular library played their content in his mind. He saw the greatness of Egypt in this desert setting. And remembered to the design of the priesthood so long ago, well mapped eons before its recorded histories in such a pattern as to continue unimpeded regardless if they were conquered and re-conquered daily. It never mattered who sat on the throne of Egypt, the evolution of their plans would never cease, and the eyes of Francis were bearing witness to that reality in this present. "And so it continues," he whispered to himself.

They were all ushered into the house by a very polite gentleman in his twenties it would appear, and quite Jewish by the look of him. He motioned for us to sit in the living room.

The inside was as mundane as the outside, well kept and clean, furnished nicely with fairly modern designed couches and chairs, but again, hardly the abode expected.

Just them an elderly gentleman entered the room, he sported a very expensive cane, but showed no real signs of needing it. He was a small framed man, dressed elegantly in a suit well tailored, he radiated his belief in well living for himself, even if not reflected in his dwelling. His hair was white and he appeared a frail man, but attuned senses told this was not so.

"I am Rabbi Kyle Burg, welcome to my humble abode. I hope your trip was pleasant. My associates are preparing food for you all, and you will be directed to sleeping accommodations after you eat. I am sure you're worn out from your long flight. If you require anything else, please alert my grandson Adam, he escorted you in here. In the meantime, I have matters requiring my attention. Francis, would you be so kind as to accompany me?"

"Of course," he said without hesitation.

The two men went into an obvious study, with a modest desk, two comfortable wing back chairs and some bookshelves built into the walls. They sat in the chairs almost facing one another.

The rabbi began to speak. "Quite some goings-on this evening, I am sorry for your losses this evening as well. Our little network stays quite informed, and unlike most of you, I must rely on simple communication devices. I am too old to begin developing my telepathic talents, besides, I like being of the old regime, I have had a charmed life, no regrets."

"I thank you also for your hospitality and generosity. Moving Sarah was imperative this evening."

"Ah Sarah, so much responsibility for such a young lady. But we are born to our destinies, are we not? Now she wanders the desert as Moses once did, same desert too."

"Personally I am not a big believer in destiny, as I feel it is the result of not taking responsibility for one's own life and direction of it. Like astrology, you need to check your stars every day only if you do not take charge of your life, letting constellational formation dictate it for you."

"Interesting take on destiny, Francis, very. I often wondered about that myself, but again, very old school here. The human race is a very superstitious one indeed, carrying even the most ridiculous ones forward in their lives. Set a ladder on a public street and even children instinctively walk around rather than under it. Our religions too, just look at this part of the world my new friend, terror, killing, wars, all over some artifacts that when found will make no difference to world stability at all, only provide new reasons to kill each other."

"We agree there. I am forty years old, and have heard the idea of 'Middle East peace' all my life, and also heard of never-ending war here. I think the greatest roadblock to peace is a general lack of interest in one."

That caused the old man to laugh out loud. "Yes, yes very true. People here want what they want, and will kill for the next ten generations to get it. Muslims, Christians, Jews all with a stake in the history of these sacred lands. Yet, such atrocity over sacred places, and such stupidity in it all."

"Sooner or later it will implode into itself here, and the sacred places will be gone, or one of the powers that claim to be will turn the Middle East to an ocean of nuclear glass, much like the plans being formulated for the United Sates I would imagine. But we cannot allow that thinking anymore, we cannot afford to look at all this and see what those that desire destruction want us to see. They want the world afraid, every day, every hour, into as many generations as possible, inherited fear, implanted into the DNA of us and our children. It is the struggle within our spiritual adepts, to rid themselves of eons of programmed fear buried deep in the very cells of them. As an alcoholic struggles with addiction, until he realizes he trying to break the addiction of every addict in his genealogical lines. The struggles power seems to make sense to them. So it is with all this superstitious belief accumulating since humans feared the moons eclipses."

"And now, we stand on the brink of total destruction and total awakening. Choices within choices, within choices. The old will not surrender, it will self destruct hoping to take as many with them as possible, it is the message of a suicide bomber, not that his God is greater, but that the belief in his God must persist, even though he knows it is done. It is his own internal desperation of what he cannot see, only sense, that causes his elation as he straps explosives to himself. He knows his God has not made a damned bit of difference to his life, his poverty, his misery, to that of his children, only that he has nothing else to believe in."

"It is our goal to make this transition without the self destruction, but as tonight has proven, old ways do not die, they kill, it is their only hold to a hope that has no hope within its substance. Children being bought and sold is an ancient tradition, just as religion is, with the same result in my opinion. Both are the rape of people's souls."

"So I can assume you'll not be attending church while you're here?"

It was Francis's turn to laugh out loud.

"No, probably not," he said, noticing it was the first smile he had felt on his lips since this all began.

"I have financed a lot of the center openings around the world, I and some friends of mine. We believe strongly that the changes we are seeing are ones that will benefit the entire world. We are in a race my friend, and the winners will be those that make the transition as your friend in the desert is doing presently."

"What she is doing is grieving, a shit load of it, I would imagine. But there is something else happening with her, something I have never seen before, an energy field like ten people. My senses tell me she will either come to terms with it out there, or not, but either way she needed someplace this vast to do it in."

"I just hope she does not run into any undesirables out there."

"Me too, God help them if she does."

XVII
Death Is Not the End

Sarah walked far into the open desert, it was a place where the Soul can commune even with the uninitiated. This evening though, she was a new species moving across the landscape of this ancient place.

Although there were many such new human beings around the world, Sarah was walking in a dimension unto herself.

Her mind was an exploding inferno of emotion, while at center was a pearl of calm and clarity beyond definition at present. Her mind seemed to be sitting within this pearl in silent meditation, while her chakras were fusing together into a single redesign of human energy potential. Energies in the human frame of skin is a wonder of containment and flow, and eternal breath.

Sarah broke into a full run, like the wind she ran across the darkened terrain with total abandon, caring not what lie beneath her feet or in her path. Her energies were carrying her faster than reality permits, achieving that point some of us do, time slows next to you parting like the sea to allow something larger than itself to pass unimpeded to its destination. Surreal space is true space, that place we finally let go of our perceptions of matter and its organization for our purposes, revealing its truest self.

Our mind knows we are countless microscopic life forms living together in an unsaid agreement to be our form. This is the birthplace of our desire for harmony, it is not a thought of enlightenment, but of our most basic survival mind saying, peace must reign or death will come. Our life lives on in spite of our constant interferences into the perfect balance the unseen lives live.

It is this awareness that Sarah ran within trying to escape herself and her minds nagging to look at the evening's events, and the loss she was carrying in a way that she would not know how to deal with. She knew she stood at the birthing moment of something that was going to live forever, and she was not prepared for any of this. Who in the name of God's darkest hell could be ready?

Sarah could feel her heart ready to explode from the exertion being put on it, finally skidding to a halt on her knees, sand flying away from her like water into the darkness. She collapsed onto her back under a sky full of stars appearing so close she could pluck them from the sky, yet she had no desire to appreciate this beauty of God's artistry. Such beauty in the midst of her feelings seemed almost a profane mockery of events in her life.

She could feel her energies calming, her blood returning to a normal rate of flow, and her body heaving less convulsively, yet her mind still rebelled against the memory of Amanda lying in her own blood, slaughtered as the sacrifice to perpetual human ignorance. Death is all the race seemed to understand as the final transition of itself, she thought. All that was sacred is shit on in this lifetime, people are pigs wearing fine linens to mask their gluttony, perfumed to hide the stench of their deliberate desire to slop in the waste of each other. So much good done to fall to such treachery for the perpetuation of rape at every level humanly possible to anything that represented purity.

Her awareness went to Angie, smiling at her death, even hoping her still alive on the way to her pain, hoping she lingered on the steps, feeling her blood flow from her until death, pondering hells awaiting as she died. Her awareness told her of Angie's childhood in suffering, yet her heart turned from the compassion, for they shared common choices within their suffering, and her choice was no choice, still a choice. "Die a thousand slow deaths, you bitch," she thought more.

"ENOUGH!" she heard screamed into her mind.

"I'll say when it is enough, and I have only begun. I hate right now, and I am deserving of its joy. Enough, indeed it is ENOUGH. I have tried to do it sanely in the midst of a race of predatory self-indulgent drama junkies. Debating is all they desire for progress, because beyond it lies real change, they fear their own shadow in it. The human race dies from apathy and laziness, rotting in their own stagnation, too fucking lazy to clean their own house, too busy raping the Earth's gifts, too busy sticking their hands in their own pants to resolve anything, men and women alike think from their crotches, all too busy blaming the other for it to even see their organs being self massaged by the very fight of it. Fight-flight-or fuck, that is the Golden Rule of this race!"

"My, that is quite a dissertation on the human condition, Sarah. Although accurate for some, did we not teach that this is not the true majority. But we deal so often with that caliber of human that we can forget ourselves, and slip into darkness. When we radiate light, it does no good to shine it where there is already light."

"What makes you the expert?"

"Is that not my body lying at that home back there?"

"Amanda, I miss you so much."

"Am I not here? Am I not talking with you, am I not comforting you?"

"I am beyond comfort in this, you can feel me, what you feel is tenacious grief, anger, hatred, it is as powerful as our love in this chasm of despair. I want that bitch Angie to rot, I want all those child fucking twisted bastards to die tonight, in a pain filled hell of the horror they brought to others."

"SO, the old man in the coffee shop was revenge then?"

"I have always wondered, could I have stopped its flow? Could I have kept him from dying? In truth, would I have? I did not regret it, I felt no remorse, as I feel none for Angie. Perhaps I just became so callous to compassion and have not realized it."

"Those are all questions beyond answering from the past. Our quest lies in the future, the very far future, born in and of the present, as we always planned our transition. Mine just came sooner."

"How did we miss her, how did she get so close and not be seen by our senses, by everyone's sense detection? Jesus, how slow were we to miss something right under our chakras? Are you a memory to me now, Amanda? A lover I will think of in later years only to drift into simu-memory for a moment?"

"Recall the last moment, on the bed. I held my consciousness alive in my body until I saw your eyes, then I jumped into your eyes. Not very accurate, but close enough for now Sarah. The pearl of calm within your torrents of emotions has been me. I am like a blue pearl in the vastness of your consciousness as we speak. Search yourself, you went to the Sea of Glass, and I was not there, all the places we travel to in energy work I am not there. I am here."

"I cannot deal with this right now as such, I have lost my childhood friend, my lover, and had to flee my home, our home, to this desert, and now I must come to terms with this. I have been patient in all of this and gone with whatever flow has been asked of me, but this is not what I desire to be wrestling with in the midst of such horrible sadness. This is insane, I mean clinically and certifiably insane."

"As we always said 'sanity is highly overrated' and as most of life's situations, we have little choice but to move along with the truth of our circumstance. Most of what we talked of and have done has been insane by a standard of sane action that cannot define itself. As we also always said, we are no fans of absolute truths. Change is where reality lies, not in the still and motionless, that is the center of death."

"Ride the waves of reality, for there is no other way to experience it. Stability is the sign of a controlled people. A clean desk is the place of the work stoppage, it is the key log in the jam. What will I do without you?"

"You have me, in a way many lovers dream of, and we have

to learn the real value of consciousness in real reality. I miss my body too, Sarah, believe me. The way it felt when you held me, made love to me, just brushed my arm as we passed each other. I cannot cry to relieve this feeling as you can, so cry, Sarah, cry until you cannot anymore for us both, so we can begin to know this new dimension. We are heading into dimensions not known. But for now we must rid ourselves of this hate, Sarah. My God, I never felt such powerful emotions in you."

"I know the hatred is death, but I feel it so strongly, as I once did for the old man, but by the time I saw him in that coffee shop, I had no such feelings, I did not feel them the day he died, but this, this is stronger than I want to feel, yet cannot stop its flow."

"Angie's life was far worse than both of ours combined. She made worse choices in the name of survival. She lived daily in the world of humans you were just ranting on about. Political correctness stifles truth, not allows it as people have been duped to believe. There are humans and there are human beings, each walk upright, but some still think on all fours, and will always fight to be the primary species in life. As you expressed, Sarah, fight, flight, or fuck. Fucking is the act of the animal human, the only way it knows to resolve its aggressive passions without harming, without killing. Prostitutes are a necessary part of the human element, they prevent murders, the illusion is that this that this is a male malady exclusively. There is the ugly truth hiding in equality."

"So where do I go now, without you by my side my beloved, without your arms to surround my fears and allow them to trail away in the feeling of you? Why did I lose you like this?"

"Why is the question of a child to stay up later. You know it will reveal itself with the journey, lest you stay in this desert forever, and we know you came out here with that intention. I live on so you may live, never alone and never without purpose, I will be with you always, Sarah."

"Why am I here in this desert? Theresa sent me here, she knows something she is not saying, so does Peter. We have brought two great conspirators together, they see into a future we cannot see yet, and Francis knows them both from another time, doesn't he?"

"Yes, they all know one another from many times, many lives, many empires, they are the ones that stood behind the thrones. Some are fixed players in this long game of evolving humans to the greatness of beings in human form, others, as Francis are the wanderers through times, lives, and aligners of the chord through time that the race pulls themselves along to the present."

"How do you know this?"

"From here I can see so much more, and know so much more clearly. Perhaps that is why we are as we are in this moment, two as one, as we have been since children, now it is just a new dimension of a fantasy we shared as little girls running along the creek laughing in simpler times, yet equally dangerous times in our life. So, are you done sending people to hell to rot and condemning the race to, how did you put it? Ah yes 'a desire to slop in the waste of each other.' My God what a great line for historians to remember you by."

"I do have my moments. Theresa would be laughing her ass off at that. This is just too sad, Amanda, just too sad. We planned it so carefully, yet let this happen, in our own home no less."

"Yes, in our own room. Plans are an assembly of variable possibilities at best, too many to know, too many to track precisely, Theresa's wise words. We did our best, and got sloppy in a false security in our environment. Forgetting security is the grand illusion. The plan that works is the one that bends with the winds of sudden change. We were too confident that we were the wind. We blew it, get over it. But we did see many children rescued, and the opening of doors of great energies coming together, believing they did so by happenstance, successes are measured in lives saved and powers merging, we succeeded my love."

"Yes, perhaps, but the price paid still enrages me. You, lying back there in that cold cellar waiting for me to say goodbye, the price is too high."

"That is not me, this is me. We cling to those ancient beliefs, and this is proof that we are not enlightened at all, only pretending until it is real enough to be called reality. Alcoholics—fake it until you make it, but know you will always be alcoholics—here is the cure, but never lose the disease, it is your life blood. Let me go so we may go together, accept that the shattering of one dream is the birth of another, I have to, please don't make me do this without you, Sarah. I have lost a lot dear to me this night also. Yet found something more wonderful. Sharing it with you, in you, makes it bearable. There is lovemaking, Sarah, greater than making love."

"My mind reels against this, it has no point of reference for this, except those points of insanity. How can two merge as one? You are you and I am me."

"And we are all together—coo coo ka choo. Sorry, no way could I let that go by. I don't know, Sarah, you don't know, I just know we will figure it our as we always have. Therein lies the only trustable reality in one that falls away in the next moment, as they always do. My murder is history now, as are the words we said a second ago. We allude ourselves to believe our words lay a foundation into the future for us to walk upon, while most fall to the ground to be blown away, the others run into themselves and create the explosions that catapult us into the action that actually move us into the future. We forget the words. Only the experience gets recorded into our cells for the next generation to decipher."

"True experience does not require language, it reveals itself as the language all life speaks, feeling is its vocal chord, the chord that connects us all. It is what connected us. All lovers feel this connection, especially in the beginning of loves power, it is why we seek it out, we know it to be the way we are designed to live, it is the goal we usher in at present. Lovers fight when they fear this feeling is leaving them, not realizing that it projects from themselves, not one another. It is up to the individual to maintain this level of awareness, even if the other does not."

"It certainly explains affairs. Seeking out the power of love's influence, it is healing and rejuvenating to mind, body, and spirit. Not realizing it is generated in the spirit of the person opening the door to vampire behaviors. People having affairs are seeking energy as the vampire seeks blood, both being life sustaining desires, along with the promise of eternal life, as measured by quality, not longevity."

"Do you see why I grieve so deeply for the loss of my lover?"

"Yes, but we had taken it to the next level already my love. All of our life came from source, we did not need each other for love, we chose each other for it, we did not complete each other, we enhance the other, growing ever stronger and larger. We did not make love, love made us, and look what it has made us now."

"Yes, look indeed. People call this being possessed. Remember 'people that hear voices have good reason to fear them' and they will fear this. I do."

"Those you are surrounded by will know and understand, perhaps even envy, those that do not sense this, will not care, wherein lies the problem? This event is a very intimate one between us, like love making, the blending of our flesh, feelings and energies. Was it not our spoken goal to achieve such one-ness that we could not tell where I started and you left off? Ta-da!"

"Simultaneous orgasm was as close as we got to this, what a rush those were, and I suppose you will not miss those?"

"Very much, but there are things of great pleasure beyond orgasm in the realm of human ability, we have just not truly allowed our minds to ponder them for fear of losing our desire for the orgasm, such as it is. Yet orgasm is tied to our primal ancestors and primal emotions. The evolved mind is blocked in its pursuit of pleasures beyond fleshly orgasm by our desire to achieve the perfect orgasm. Fucking as human desire is the whip that tames the beast, making love desires a more evolved mind, yet reverts to the primal screams of orgasm inevitably. We demand our lovers be refined and evolved in lovemaking, yet also demand they be primal and take us to the prime evil forests again with unbridled passions and raw emotional lust. This is a very uncomfortable paradox men suffer in these times, the demands of women that see themselves as trophies to be sought, yet sue you if you act as they demand. They want whores in the bedroom and 'Mr. Mom' in the living room, helping with the kids and able to cook."

"Women walk a sharp sword these days, one that feels oddly familiar from a long ago past. Myth of matriarchal leadership from times not recorded."

"Remember your history, I know you can recite the male Pharos by name and lineage, how many female Pharos are written into those books? There were many of them, from Nubian all through Egyptian, yet the history lies destroyed with deliberate malice. The same precedence are being repeated in this time. Spirituality has become female dominated, with few male teachers being given credence or recognition. Men are being devalued to represent equality of women. Both see it, yet lack answers to its dichotomous nature. Priests have repeated their mistakes of the ancient world, so the pendulum keeps swinging, cutting us all as it passes. Unless they both resign from the conflict, it will end as it always has, with violent rebellion as in the old empires, setting humanity back again and again."

"Electing a woman president will be viewed as a sign of progress of civilization, yet it will just be a rerun of the same old, same old. Mistakes leapfrogging through time, to the same dead ends. Within it lies a boredom that would make God yawn, and does make the human race impotent to their own desires, hours of pumping and no orgasm, until frustration becomes a violent convulsion demanding release. Much like religion is experiencing at present. Centuries of bliss promised and no orgasm of divine stroking ever occurred."

"Civilization is a limp penis, and there is no Viagra for it, brought on by the woman's demand for more and better orgasm, until the man just doesn't give a damn about her pleasure anymore. She has screamed so long for her pleasures, she has become the creature that thinks with its clitoris. Love never even entering into the equation of resolution. When she is a bitch, she just says the man has issues with strong women, as men lay claim to dominance as a male right."

"It is easier for men and women to masturbate to pleasant fantasies than try to meet all demands of being a lover anymore, and civilization has taken the same course of reaction to its frustrations. War being the convulsive response to many centuries of trying to achieve orgasm for itself. Religion is still masturbating, with a limp penis, but the frustration of non fulfillment is exploding in rage, not divine bliss."

"We are the love entering into the equation, but it is not having the desired response, because it is still being measured as sexual fulfillment, not emotional power over all of this. The race has masturbated with vibrators for so long, it fears not having them anymore. We took Angie's vibrator from her, so she self destructed, after taking out the ones she blamed for the theft."

"Pretty fucked up, huh? We were the living picture of love

she never believed possible from being so jaded all her life, looking at us expressing the degree of how we feel was forcing her to see the vibrator as the addiction it is. Society cannot afford not have people addicted to their pleasure organs. I was killed for envy, leaving your happiness destroyed, and the equation unfixable in her mind. But things being what they are, she only pushed it to the next level, and this will be her hell, knowing it, because be assured my beloved, she knows now. Listen into the cosmos, you can hear her screams."

"So we just keep on building anew within the old, and those that cannot stop stroking themselves will self-destruct, self extinction. Becoming future fertilizer for the Earth and generations to feed from, like the dinosaurs. Neanderthals did not die off, they walk amongst us, with political correctness preventing showing them to be that, they can only be seen by their actions, like the old man that raped me daily, and your parents raping you daily with Jesus. But navigation without triggering the self destruction is imperative, is it not?"

"What makes it imperative is the desire to escape our guilt for it, we seek to escape our own programmed emotions, if we do not confront them we will recreate this all over again. Look at you, Sarah, my love, out here in this desert alone in the sand, driven here by the conflict of the programmed reaction to the circumstances of my death, and the response of this as you actually feel it. All those emotions raging out of you were placed there across generations into your DNA, your cells are raging at your true emotions, because if you do not honor the programmed input, they will die. Your mind has accepted my death, your heart is aching for real, but you know this is a far superior way to address all of this, and one that promises fruition of those things we talked of all of our lives."

"It still sucks big time, anyway you cut it, it's still a shit pie for me to ingest."

"That's disgusting, Sarah, but true. You are smiling though love, and that makes me feel alive again as I was just a short while ago."

"Although I agree with all this, and this new 'situation' shall we call it, I cannot help it, Amanda, right now I want to hold you so badly. I feel so empty somehow."

"Lay back and close your eyes, my beloved."

Sarah did as she was asked. She lay back onto the sand, feeling it shift to caress her form.

She looked at the stars for a few seconds as she slowly closed her eyes. Her body began to feel warm from within, from a depth her mind had not charted yet. She felt her awareness somehow moving towards the warmth, as the energy of two lovers approaching one another, feeling the emotions begin to swell within them, feeling the pace of their approach was quickening. The warmth filled her now, and began to caress her from inside as Amanda's arms once did, she could feel the feelings flow outside of her now and wrap her like a layer of new skin that was there to protect and soothe her. Every atom within her was responding with the same desire as her entire body, surrender was the only possible response to this feeling. Sarah was lost in the feelings as when she and Amanda would make love in an all consuming desire of total trust and love. Her nipples began to rise and her breathing became deep. Her whole body was writhing on the desert floor in a passionate desire no source could be seen for. She felt the energy form a mystical hand designing across her vagina, and invisible fingers penetrated her full awareness, her clitoris was rising to meet a hunger that was formed of pure energy. The ecstasy began to fill her entire body as if it had become the vagina that was being penetrated and pushing against the hardness of pure desire. Every atom was alive with this erotic experience, and every cell began to scream in the orgasm that filled the deserts otherwise quiet solitude. Sarah was undulating in pure ecstatic bliss from the inside and screaming in absolute fulfillment of desires she could not have imagined in her deepest and mostly loving thoughts. She convulsed one final time for what felt hours from inside this experience, than collapsed back onto the deserts sands unaware of the saturation that flowed from her through her clothes onto the deserts disbelief of this human ability. She fell into a sleep of pure calm, still feeling her lover's unseen love wrapped around her like a blanket without seam.

"See, my beloved Sarah, there are pleasures far beyond the flesh that can command the flesh to new heights of awareness of itself. Love is the master teacher of such lessons, and every atom receives its blessings. Sleep my love, and awaken with no anger anymore. When you return to the house in the morning, I want to be cremated, and my ashes spread across the waves of the Nile River, I want it to sleep at home, where it began. I love you, my dear Sarah."

XVIII
Desert Dreams

Sarah awoke still lying in the sands as the evening had left her. She was awakened by the sight and sound of a large bird flying overhead blocking the morning sun as it passed over her. She let her mind wander the many millions that had slept under this same sky, awakening to the same natural sounds as this. She remained still for a long time until finally stirring to rise herself up. She stretched her muscles and brought them into alignment for the walk back. As she began to move she was reminded of the way she had fallen asleep, the great tremors that had shook her from the inside created by a dream she had had of her Amanda.

"That was no dream, my dearest," she heard echoing inside her mind.

So, this is real. As she began to walk, dampness against her thighs attested to her realities of the evening before. The sun was bright and the heat was returning to the desert swiftly as she let things roll across her mind's eyes. She felt rested as she had not felt in months, her energies were calm again and the inferno had ceased. Yet she knew that her energies were markedly different, and that the differences would be detected immediately upon her arrival, and explanations would be sought.

She began her trek back to the house where they had landed the night before. Night creatures were slithering and scurrying back to the safety of their holes and crevices in the sparse rocks, while the day creatures flew and scampered about in hopes of grabbing a meal of those heading for sleep. Right now her fondest hope was a large meal and shower.

"Good morning, Sarah," she heard in her being.

Sarah did not respond, still preferring the silence of her grief to the sounds of her dead lover's voice as a part of her being. The mind was not accepting of this, and her fears played a tune of caution accompanied by images of hypodermic needles filled with restful comas injected by doctors posing as healers. The world of the living dead.

She focused on the sound of her feet hitting the sand as she moved, falling into a Zen meditation of it, becoming hyper aware of each particle sliding across the others, and back to the silence of internal depth. With each exercise, awareness grew in its parameters of each. This restored her balance of herself, yet made her more acutely aware of the changes within her.

Love had made her who she was, not the pain and regrets of the past. Most abused people stay in the past until they are given their revenge, or an apology, even staying there for the purpose of recreating it. Sarah had often heard the best revenge was a happy life, but how could one possibly find happiness when its birthing thoughts were of revenge.

She had also heard revenge was a dish best served cold. She agreed whole heartedly with this, if you are going to seek revenge, serve it with a heart cold and precise, whatever you decide, do it with all your being. Even Angie knew this.

Theresa and Sarah once had a conversation regarding human abilities. No one ever did anything badly, perhaps not according to someone's specific directions, but even the worst screw up on the planet was doing it with exceptional ability. Serial killers were extraordinary predators, sexual predators genius at manipulation of the adults surrounding the children, and more criminals get away with their deeds than are caught, those in prison ingenuously arranged incarceration in lieu of committing worse crimes. So there is really no human on the planet doing anything with any sort of mediocrity, even a lazy couch potato expresses a genius at not doing any at all, or at least the very minimum.

This was where the choice was made to pursue excellence in their training and result, then to kick it higher after feeling they had achieved their goals. Last night was the kicker. Taking it beyond the possible perception of reality, to become God of her own internal universe and to allow her authority to be the one that her universe was commanded by.

More so after the loss of Amanda than ever before. She wanted to talk to Peter and Theresa about what they had found out, about that night after being taken out of the picture. Her heightened senses had pieced it together, so the conversation would be one of affirmation, not information.

She could see the house now, and the pole barn holding the jet they had come here in.

She also knew that Francis had been following her for some time now at what he thought to be a fair distance. He had followed her footsteps in the sand beginning around dawn.

Another strange side effect was that she slept soundly enough, very satisfied in her emotional state, but remained aware of her surroundings for a greater distance and deeper truth of accuracy. Was this hers, or Amanda enhancing her ability? It mattered not, it was a reality.

Sarah stopped and looked over the rocks to the west of her, cupped her hands and yelled loudly. "Come out, Francis, come and walk with me please."

She awaited a response, which came quickly as he appeared from a formation of large stones. He walked in her direction. Strange man this Francis, a powerful energy to be certain, but one even the most seasoned empaths and psychics seemed to steer clear of.

It was not fear, nor any negative emotion, it was just something that came into the room with him. He and Peter knew each other, their paths having crossed over their lives, both men of mystery yet totally open when in your presence. Theresa and Francis had worked closely together over the last few years preparing the Cleveland center and the operation of a few nights ago. His affiliation with the monks had proven to be a great gift in all of this.

He said he lived with them, but he was never there, he just simply showed up when needed and when he said he would be there. He had reached her.

"You are well, Sarah." It was a statement, not a question.

"Yes, I am, thank you. I sense Theresa sent you out into the desert in the middle of the night."

"Who else would ask such a thing?" he said with a wry smile.

Sarah returned the smile. "She is such a mother hen, but God knows many love her for just that quality, myself included."

"I sense you have come to terms with the death of your friend and lover. I am sorry, Sarah, I truly am. Everything happens for a reason they say, but 'they' seldom know what they are talking about. We however do know of what we speak, or we do not speak."

"They, a euphemism for the people that killed her. 'They' have been running the world for far too long, and it is time for it to end, my friend."

"Oh? We're going to conquer the world now? My, you are pissed!"

"No, not anymore actually, I was, but that has passed. I want to tend to Amanda's body. I know now why Theresa sent me here with her. We are going to cremate her and then send her ashes down the Nile, it is what she wanted. Life goes on, Francis."

"That it does, my friend. I brought some food along in case you were hungry."

"Famished actually. Do you mind if we sit and eat, I am very hungry and a little tired."

"Not at all, it'll give us a chance to talk. We never really have, always so busy and all. It was a great tragedy losing

Amanda that way. I understand the operation was successful globally though. Such things have been a part of the human landscape since the dawn of time. Yet we stand on the brink of eradicating most of it for the first time in history. It would be nice, wouldn't it?"

"Beyond nice. It is always a matter removing the reasons of justification of it. War will live on until peace becomes more profitable. Child selling will live on until the world views itself differently. But you already know all of this, don't you?" she said, biting a sandwich and glaring into his eyes.

"I know some things, I suppose," he replied, looking off into the distance.

"You know Peter and Theresa, you knew Peter before I did. They say you live with the monks in the Cleveland Ashram, but no one can ever reach you there. You just seem to show up when you're needed."

"I stay busy."

"God's above! Doesn't anybody in this new era just say what they mean, be who they are, state what is the truth? Everyone is a fucking mystery, chasing mysteries and trying to be so illusive you can't even see them. We're all wearing spiritual camouflage, and no one sees who we are."

"Yeah, true, tell me, Sarah, being out in the open, how's that working for you and Amanda? Going to work, school, even the grocery store, passing someone that is about to get hit by a car, their child is being abducted, their husband will have a heart attack in two days, telling them, how is that working out for everyone?"

"Like shit and you know it. I have a dead best friend to prove your point. People died to help kids we knew were in trouble, and where. Now the people that should have been saving them are looking for us, because they perceive *us* as some threat. That's how it's working out."

"Yes, thought so. So what then? What do we do? I mean The Secret is out, *The Celestine Prophecy* is out in the open, the

Bible has been published, and yes, it's true, Buddhism has come to America."

"What is your point, smart ass?"

"I have no point. Just a perspective, like you. Jesus knew what he was doing, as did Buddha and the rest, they knew it would take until now for things to evolve. But everyone is trying to be some sort of mystique walking around in their lives, telling everyone their mind, their secrets, to warn them of impending doom. We believe anything that is printed in a book, on the Internet, channeled, spoken in a spiritual bookstore. People are walking around with crystals and gems shoved up their asses, because some psychic at a fair told them to cleanse themselves by doing it. Pray to this God, meditate with a Toyota on your forehead, smell this, burn that, draw a pentagram on your house for protection, and watch them set your house on fire."

"I get that, I really get it now. I set myself up for this."

"Yes, you did, but there was no stopping you, so people were brought in to protect you as best we could, and to continue the original ideas. You crossed a bridge in that coffee shop when you projected your emotion through your chakras like that. It was a sign that the evolution had reached an apex. You were not the only one, there were others around the world also, some more recently, and some previous to you. Out there last night, I think you crossed another bridge, right, Amanda?"

"She said right."

"Of course she did. Scary stuff?"

"Yes, but not scary as you right now. You are as frightening to me as her inside of me, people that can recall their lineage to its beginnings are scary, Francis. No one knows if it is true or their just making it up as they go with enough historical information to make it seem credible. But sensory enhancement tells me it is true."

"Everyone has this ability, they carry the memories within.

The whole body is the product and the home of mind. You know that, as do most people in these times, they just see no reason to delve into it, they cannot see the practicality to its use in the present, except to clear unpleasant memories from the present. You have not explored this part of yourself, so you fear it."

"I am an empath, I have enough to deal with just processing sensory energies in the course of a day."

"Empath is a word for the newest fad of spiritual marketing, and what will be 'in' next after Reiki and whatever else sells books and workshops to the searching. You will not know what you are until you stop calling yourself anything. Words like empath are used to make others comfortable, not you. Tell me you do not feel a twinge in your solar plexus every time you say the word."

"I do, but so much has been punching my solar plexus lately, a twinge is a welcomed relief. You, Theresa, and Peter, you know the future, don't you?"

"No, we do not, Sarah, no one sees it, it is full of variables that can send it off in directions unseen and not thought of. Like prophecies, they could only see a behavioral pattern in the web of human fabric and predict where that particular behavior would take them, change the behavior and the prophecy is voided."

"Yet so many seem to be reality now."

"Because so many believe them across so many generations, they lie like sleeping ancestors in your cells, and they have been programmed to awaken now, and awaken they have. Muslims, Christians, Jews, the big three. They will bring about the destruction of entire civilizations because they have prophecies screaming in their DNA right now. This is something that the world has not taken seriously enough yet, but it will soon."

"What is the value of knowing all your past lives then?"

"It is not about past lives, it is about knowing all of yourself as a single life, not one here and one there, not trying to put a puzzle together. It is being aware of all there is to be aware of within ourselves, the good, the bad, and the wondrous. It is something that occurs unconsciously all the time in everyone's life. Most of our lives run on an automatic assimilation of information between the past and the present, a constant flow from the beginning to present, because time does not exist, it is all the same life."

"It serves to fulfill that spiritual New Age phrase we have heard so much, one of wholeness, totality, oneness. One of those phrases that everyone repeats, searching for its meaning. Wholeness is so many aspects of human life. Health, wealth, peace of mind, so many ideals."

"When I read a lot, I read to remember, to awaken those experiences locked within. We are the Akashic records we seek in the sands. I read to learn things in my own time, yet it always felt as though I was studying to catch up on what had transpired while I was gone. Now—you Sarah, carry the consciousness of two. It will be interesting to see what will come of this development in your growth."

"Yes, will I be two as one? I don't think such answers will come for a while. I hear her and you simultaneously, multidimensional awareness. It seems easy, yet the mind tries to perceive it as difficult, trying to find ground for reason and purpose for all this change."

"Dimension is generally accepted as degrees of freedom, the parameters we feel safe within. Generally those we were born to. Yet once the lineage of ones life is truly realized, operating in multi dimensions seems natural, and therein lies the value of knowing yourself across all time. It is also a necessity for living in a universe that does not always honor our definitions of time and space."

"Universal migration, the human race moving into galactic settlements."

"It is the reason for the conditions as they are here at

present. Everything seems to be pointing to the end. 'End of Times' as the religionists say, and they are surely accurate in that prophecy. As with the calamity that your changes have wrought in your life, it is a miniature version of what is occurring on a global basis. Spirituality teaches that we are all one, all connected. 'Before Abraham was, I am' so it is only natural that individual growth and that of large populations, and the world mimic each other. It is the same movement, the same motion. The old that will not ride the changes will choose death, or create circumstances that will end their days. Religions are not at war, they are suicidal."

"Back to the original topic, Francis, what now? After I tend to Amanda's body, I have no clue as to what is next for myself, the center, any of it."

"Be honest, have you ever known what was next? From your childhood to the other evening, have you actually known what was next? Did you know what you were going to do when you left the coffee shop with Peter that day? Synchronicity comes from internal attraction, not some universal hand moving the players around on the Earths surface like a board game. You drew Peter to that shop, and he responded, and the old man. You had decided that it was done, you needed to leave it behind and you began the energy amassing of closure, the coffee shop was that manifestation. Even the actual way it went down was a fantasy of yours, tell me I am wrong."

"I see why Theresa trusts you so well, and why she sent you along. Honesty of self is usually ascribed to something negative within. Amanda and I learned to seek out the positive in one another. It was something totally new to us, like this. Now there is in life a new trend to focus on our strengths and our attributes."

"Well, as I understood the plan, we should be into phase two in a couple of days. Depending on you of course, and how you are feeling with all of this. The kids rescued are being given a couple of days to acclimate, then we hit the TV screens with them all, correct?"

"Yes, that was the plan and I see no reason for it to change. It's time people sitting at home saw the carnage, and the kids emotions are raw enough to state what they feel. American TV will eat it up."

"To be sure they will. As will most of the other countries. The kids from the more volatile eastern countries are being brought here to Israel for televising, it's about as neutral as it gets over here. The Muslim countries will deny the access, or use it as a propaganda tool to try and swing it back on western culture. Christian reporting is being denied on our end, for fear of the same thing, these kids have been used enough."

"Religious Zealots on all ends will have to find their own martyrs. Is Theresa arranging to have the local kids moved to the Cleveland center?"

"As we speak I am sure. She has made an Interpol connection, a woman named Maria. The woman also came with a CIA clone that was supposed to return with you in tow. Peter and some of the monks sent him away very unhappy and extremely pissed off. They gave him a demonstration of energy over mind, he is not going to take this well, and I would presume, he knows where you are."

"How could he? I have not been here even a day?"

"The assumption he does is a safer thought pattern, Sarah. One that you should have adopted at the center. Assume they know, assume they are in the next room. Because they do, and they are, like Angie was. These people have been training on a parallel path with us, no one ever said these abilities are for the righteous. God reigns down on good and evil alike. Believe it, Sarah. Angie was well trained, it is how she slipped under your radar. The race is on, and we have to accelerate our training of everyone. Let the 'Starchildren' play with the Indigos, we cannot afford such airy fairy approaches to change."

"The time for workshops and meetings on Sunday night are past, I feel it in every fiber of my being. The Dalai Lama asking those monks to work alongside this is a sign we have entered a critical phase of transition in the world. The old is beginning to implode in on itself, and the old money is running scared. The Arab league is looking at their hold on oil being devalued by new technologies, rendering their hold on the world unstable."

"Yes, well that's all well and good, but meetings of the oil Czars is being directed to take hostage any new technology that comes to light. The question was posed to them. 'Do you want to be oil Czars? Or energy Czars?' It was much like a meeting of the old Hitler regime with the same domination of the world at stake in their minds, just a different type of atrocity, this one is legal and morally acceptable 'free enterprise.' Gotta love majority apathy, number one killer of humans."

"Wow, powerful analogy, but it feels right on the money, no pun intended. But we will deal with that later, right now I want to tend to Amanda."

"I have been sensing her chattering in your ear, so to speak right along. Very opinionated entity."

"You have no idea. This is going to take some getting used to."

"You'll adapt to it. It is just integral realities of consciousness. She is not 'inside' you per se but until we adjust to multi dimensions as our real time reality as we experience this one, it will feel abrasive to your mind. But considering what she meant to you, I would think you would welcome this experience, such as it is."

"I do, but I don't. I have not been responding to her this morning, I need time to sort this out in my one experience. I can feel it, and you're correct, it feels abrasive to the mind, but I do not want it to leave me. I hear her talking to me, yet it is coming from a different source within me. Can you explain this?"

"She is communicating through new avenues opening your mind. Your mind is being governed differently from the pituitary acting now as 'commander and chief' over the integration of the new DNA coding, unified chakras, and the unfolding of your subconscious into the conscious. In short, you're becoming whole. The constant chatter from her consciousness is necessary to keep the unfolding in motion, and she is not offended by your lack of response. This is the goal of meditation as well, meditation being evolved by choice and deliberate action, you're being quantum leaped by experiences within circumstances."

"*So* while we're all experiencing this differently, we're all experiencing a common experience."

"Or not."

"Amanda is not a part of me then, but she can communicate as if she was right here. She maintains her own consciousness, and I my own. Yet they both co-exist in the same field of consciousness. 'And the dead shall rise.'"

"Ah prophecy again. God, save me from your followers. It is a simple yet accurate analogy though. It is wholeness, simple enough to accept. So many 'movements' in our time distract from this reality trying to creep into our lives. Christianity was the world's greatest distraction from the quest of wholeness, as are many religions. They pull our attention from internal integration to a deity outside our reach as human beings. Circumstance forced you to reach beyond yourself and your programmed beliefs, because we do not have to be honoring them for them to be influencing our lives."

"Amanda's love for me was so strong she pushed it beyond the limit at her death to stay with me, refusing to just go, and accept death as she was programmed to believe in it. The power of love has even begun to be realized."

"Nor has its true nature."

"No, I suspect not. But we are well on our way. Theresa sent you with me to help me assimilate this new awareness with Amanda?"

"Of course. More precisely she sent me to help you adjust to this all, if you required it, she did not anticipate Amanda's jump of her own awareness, but our greatest moments are the ones that present us life or death choices. We have gotten reports from other people from that evening making quantum leaps in skills occurring. Even making guards put down their weapons by telepathic commands. Amazing times, Sarah, yet desired."

"Amazing times indeed, Francis."

XIX
Goodbyes

Amanda's body burned atop a wooden platform in the desert night, illuminating a darkness accustomed to its absolute dominance of light. A ten-foot circular fire line had been set around the platform to deter any desert creatures from getting to curious of this ceremony. Sarah sat with Francis atop a ridge looking down on it, the site was one that would burn into their memories, the great fire within the circle, as ancient of a sight as there could be in this isolation.

Francis sat wondering how many ancient memories would awaken to this ritual, feeling the funerary emotions such a sight produced. Time bowed its presence to obscurity unable to fix itself in a particular frame of itself, letting human desire take precedence over its demands.

Sarah was in deep meditation, communing with Amanda, an honorable and loving space to witness the loss of one's flesh. Within the sacredness of her silence, they were one in sorrow of what was, and an elation of that which is new. A condition Francis felt the world would be experiencing soon enough. He was appreciating this lapse in times demands, like a respite within the hurricane of changes.

In her place of feeling and heart Sarah's soul was in silent undulation with Amanda's soul.

Swimming as two waters in a single pond, other life swimming about them, only the water aware of itself. Here is where the mourners gathered also. This also was apart of the new paradigm. The flesh being consumed in the simple reality of the flames, tears left to the old ways of life ending when the flesh ceased to be.

Around the pond of swirling emotion, now forming a lake

of feeling in a field of energy we have embraced as home finally, stood Peter, Theresa, scores of workers and visitors of the center, monks adding a sacred veil of light, all those that knew and understood what these women strove for in this life. In a simple meditation a gathering of souls appear in the field of the universe to be sanctified and honored as the great creations they are, after millenniums of self debasement and seeking only the darkest corners of their imagination.

From this place a laser of hope will seek everyone that is opened to themselves as the universes wondrous selves, citizens of a new ideal larger than self. As the undulation of these two souls continued, more and more souls appeared around them, all those in the past and the present came to pass in the realization that the human race had finally come of age. Above them a light formed of the ones that had died to the flesh that same night as a ray from the center reached upward to touch them. A statement being made to the those alive and asleep that time was now theirs to command and to direct, and the path chosen was one of survival into living. This is the place of unity, of interconnectedness so long sought, the place where all converse, never to be interrupted. What stood over here and walked over there no longer know the difference. No up or down, here or there, all is one, let the minds that grasp embrace, those that cannot, let them sleep the sleep of history.

Francis stayed focused on the light at the funeral fires center, as his eyes felt the centuries fall away and he welcomed all those that had stood in such a feeling. Around the fire for miles into miles the spirits of the ancients stood in fixed fascination of the flames that carried Amanda's cells with the wind, he felt them carried into the universe wishing them a safe journey to the next galaxy that would one day find a beautiful young blonde human running the landscapes of a new world not yet known. That is the way of this creation we call human, should ignorance win out in this time, the cells of us all blown into oblivion will land in some distant galaxy, and we will grow again from the ashes, even on yet unborn worlds, every atom a Phoenix. To spite our greatest efforts to worship mortality, we are eternal. We will inhabit all the universe, one way or the other.

The eyes wander in such openness and vastness. He had often heard the desert and oceans were reminders of how small we are in the grand scheme. Francis was feeling quite the opposite, larger out here, standing taller, feeling deeper without trepidation of what feelings may arise, confident that being human was a good choice for living a life. To look out into the nothing and see no thing artificially created has a calming effect it sets into motion and a remembering catalyst, consciousness reaches into its past as far the desert's horizons. It is not a memory, but a re-experiencing of the moments, totally ignoring the parameters of our minds demands on times limitations.

Off in the distance, the moon's light embraced the ground, stillness screamed its desire for it, its emotion demanding sameness on life entering. Francis could see wind kicking up the sand, holding it awhile in its self, then releasing it back as we often do. Swirls of sand rose from the stillness and surrounded unseen form, human form walking as they had somewhere in the great I AM, being someone before they were I AM. Such phenomenon occurs in other memories simultaneously of great whirlwinds of snow in the forests creating shapes, mighty essences looking you in the eyes reflecting snow lined nothingness as one peers into them. You hear eternity speaking directly to you. In such frames of life, one can only let their soul have voice.

Jesus walked this sand, he recalled to the present. Jesus had once said, "Do not go into the past, always call it forward, to walk in memories is like walking on the ocean floor, looking for a way home." Feeling the words resonate from his atoms to awareness in this night. "This is your life, going into the past robs you of the present, calling it to you rewards you in the same present." A little something Jesus learned from the Druids, before they sent him away for teaching everyone sacred texts. A little "something—something" he did a lot. It got him crucified eventually. I don't care who you are, crucifixion is not fun.

This is religion, spirituality, enlightenment in all their deepest desire for human beings and themselves, this is the only goal of any of it, in any form or philosophy, to feel this embrace, is all it is about, there is nothing else where "the path" leads. The mind plays Jesus walking in its eye, and flowing spirit enlarges to embrace Christ, we stand as the same, knowing the memories of Jesus, as Jesus is the memories in self. This is Christ, where Jesus and Francis are the same in a oneness called Christ, where the race stands, if it chooses to stand fully erect. Our ancestors and their current cousins can stand upright, yet return to all fours when presented with the unknown. The powers of this world have dropped to their fours, governments are circling the watering holes, watching religion drinking with their faces into the water, while global conglomerates plot to control the water. Spiritualism is threatening to poison the water, or at least convince everyone it is.

When this occurs, those standing truly erect can see one another over the backs of all those looking at the ground.

Francis turned his awareness to the funerals purpose again, still the spirits were intertwined, still the essences gathered, it was in the world now, wherever connections by knowledge and purpose were joined. Funerals for the others were scheduled for the same evening, many spirits around the world had joined in this. Francis always thought it odd, that so many people would talk about interconnectedness of all life, and equally, try to discredit those that actually walk in this reality. If you do not want something to actually enter your life, do not ponder it. Pondering occurs within that which you are thinking, it is the effortless flow we feel behind our thoughts, the winds that carry them forward to consciousness. Minds are oceans, millions of thoughts swimming by, schools of them, most beautiful, some predatory and dangerous for they eat the beautiful ones. The water holds the ponderings of the ocean where the wonder is birthed. At this thought he was with Sarah and Amanda's ponderings. Still sitting on the hill in meditation, Sarah and Amanda were feeling the way of this new union. There is nothing new about this, only that we can participate within it as we have our day to day world, it is an expansion into a new dimension that has co-existed with us always. The spiritual movement of the last century was in error in its perception that theirs was a matrix separate from the ancient one, that new meant the old existed elsewhere and not connected to them within the matrix of energies.

Sarah and Amanda were becoming new lovers once again, within the essences of themselves. Funeral rights were now a honeymoon in an entirely new vastness of intimacy.

Here "all things shall be known" and not judged. Freedom defines itself anew in this realm, and fear cannot breathe in this atmosphere. Most epiphanies are not accompanied by words of glorious dialogue, it is usually something more along the lines of "OH- SHIT!"

As David probably uttered when he first set eyes on Goliath when he got up close and personal with his reality. Thoughts of being blessed and chosen crumble to "I AM fucked" and the mind pushes violently beyond known to seek out truly new, for its salvation cannot be found anywhere else. So too the undulation of Sarah and Amanda was just such a violent push into new dimension, for there love is so strong, it refused death, pushing into a new form of life's ability to know eternity in the present. Is this into the "moment" spirit bragged of for so many centuries? The dimension sought was always there, this was just a welcoming ceremony into its awareness by human and God. As the many humans are one, the One God is the many human. In such an equation one realizes that God needs humans to exist, as humans need God to exist. Such is the river of life we navigate.

Francis stood, leaned over Sarah's meditating body, kissed her on the crown of her head and whispered, "Time to go." The last embers of Amanda's body could be seen glowing in the dark before dawn. Sarah stood and looked towards the ashes of her friend, then one tear fell from her cheek. Francis watched it roll off her skin and followed it to the ground, hearing in hyper awareness the last ember of Amanda hiss and cool with the tears landing in the sand. It is done. "Such perfection in the face of seemingly gross imperfection," he thought to himself.

As they made their way down the slopes to the funeral area, the monks were already putting Amanda's ashes into a vessel to present to Sarah. As they reached them, nothing of the evening's ceremony remained save the monk holding the jar. Francis studied Sarah as she accepted the jar from the man, kissing his cheek as she did. He was scanning her deeply, and she knew it, allowing it, for she knew what he sought. Men like Francis and Peter do not recall what a person looks like, only what they felt in their presence, they know people by their energies not their form, for this is form to them. Francis sought the changes in Sarah's form.

She walked back to Francis with the jar in hand, it was a beautiful dark blue with gold flowering all over the outer layer radiating an air of royal elegance.

"Fitting container for such a person I think," Francis said gently.

"Yes, I think so too," she said. "I hear you arranged for it, thank you."

"You are quite welcome. Does Amanda approve?"

"I will ask her when I feel her again. She has moved onto explore for a while. Yet I need only think of her and she is present."

"Then the question should make her present."

"No, actually it is the emotion within the thought that she responds to. She feels what I feel, but I am my own vessel of feeling, she is her own now also. I find it difficult to ascribe words to, but know it completely within myself. After the shooting we were as one in the confusion of the originality of it, but after this experience, we know who we are and the abilities we have within it. She is seeking out her brother, from an obvious vantage point now, but she has much to learn of her circumstance also."

"The blending of your essences seemed the zenith of a beautiful human experience, such as it was. The almost perfect way to handle transition of this sort."

"Yes, it was, sadness just did not exist within it, only love and oneness. Fear was not present either, letting someone know you so completely is freeing and liberating in a way that defies explanation. I understand you and Peter, and how you perceive people now as energy form, not fleshly impressions. Theresa and I will work on this when I return also. Amanda was at peace with this transition also, even elated, as am I. It brought to light the over importance we put on form, and the reality it is an expression of the mind into reality. Reality as we define it, is but a blank canvas we project everything onto. We have had no idea how greatly we create in every moment. Thoughts are actions from this perspective. We erroneously define the movement of our arm as the action, when in truth it is the thought to move it that is the actual action."

"We are God, self divided into billions of pieces, complete in each. For some that thought is blasphemy and salvation for others. This is working in real time because we believe it is, and a belief is thought practiced. We are not working on it, studying, or awaiting our total healing to live this, we are doing so with all of our human flaws intact. Healing is hoax, a ruse, a vicious lie. Someone miraculously cured of cancer is the healer, not the spiritual person claiming to have done it.

Healers, energy workers can aid in it but the healing is up to the person. Being God is the ultimate truth, because our definitions of God are so poor to begin with."

"Yes, that is as close to a defining ideal we will get unless we actually experience the familiarity of it. We are able to receive knowledge directly from the light we speak of so often of, we simply need to sit in stillness to let it process in us and begin to apply it in life."

"Yes, well that will come into play soon enough. I assume you'll be leaving here for Egypt. Theresa has been in touch with me, Saunders, the CIA man is arriving in Tel Aviv tonight, so you're on the road as soon as we return to the plane. Your bags are already packed and loaded."

"I am not worried about him."

"Hey, tune in here. Theresa and Peter took care of the church and all of its predators, but the CIA is hot onto you. You're a trophy for this guy, and he means to claim it, in the name of America, honor and duty. Seems they are well into this change as well, but from a different view, still the world domination scenario. Whoever has the most continents at Armageddon wins. They will use Angie's death as a murder frame to manipulate you, if they get their hands on you."

"How did he tune in so quickly?"

"You're a lot more powerful than when you left, their empaths are hard at work and you're an easy target right now. You have to develop your cloaking skill's quickly within yourself. Ask Amanda to throw an energy field over you from her domain, just until you can get it skilled for yourself. Peter said this guy is pretty skilled himself, he tangled with him at the church and sent him off really pissed off."

"God, when will this end?"

"It will end when it ends. From your experience this evening, I am sure you realize that the main reason for the hostility is that the world is trying to either stay in an old archetype, or feel they are ushering one in, but it is already in place, everyone is out of sync with time and dimension. Calendars are becoming useless now, but the clocks keep ticking in a cycle totally artificial and equally out of sync."

"Yes, I get that now, in a very real way. Everyone is on the 2012 prophecy clock, but that is not when it begins, that is when it is done. For everyone in this, it has been 2012 all of their lives."

"Exactly. This CIA guy thinks he can sop it by taking the players out of commission or manipulating them into trying to change it altogether. Once the human race is universe bound, the sources of new energy will take the wind right out the current energy Czar's sails."

"That is another story for another time I suppose. Until we develop technology to raise us into space without fossil fuels, we will remain in a mode of it being too expensive, and under government control. Private enterprise is developing finally into a competition for the governments. If this does not open to commercial space travel, the Earth will be surrounded in space stations of weaponry. We will be caught in the ultimate standoff for total world domination."

"True enough, but this shift is throwing off agendas all over the planet, add global warming and climate change, governments will be too busy with indigenous populations. Obviously the Earth is in tune with this shift also, so we have that on our side."

"Who will be accompanying to Egypt?"

"Several of the monks, basically the party you arrived here with. You'll be safe enough, just do not tarry in Egypt, there will be people from our center in Cairo meeting you there as well, they have arranged the ship to take you to the Nile and accompany you."

"And you, Francis? Where are you going?"

"I have an undertaking in Amsterdam to attend to, personal really. I am meeting an old friend there, Gwendolyn. She will be running a gathering in Holland of 'light workers' of the New Age variety. She is not aware I will be there, and not happy with my dialogue I am sure. But she always says to speak your truth, so I shall."

"I am going to Cleveland after Egypt. I will meet Peter and Theresa there at the new center. I have decided to move there permanently. The work at the college is done for me. The center runs itself and the child find will continue with a great deal of enthusiasm in Amanda's memory."

"I have spoken to them, they are of the same mind. Quarters are arranged for all of you there, and your things have been sent there as well. New start, new place, new undertakings. The global conclave there is a month off, and there is much to do for everyone's arrival. I also learned the buildings between the center and the Monastery have been acquired, so it has grown to three city blocks now. Plan on taking over the whole city?"

"Yes."

"Indeed?"

"Yes, indeed," Sarah said with a disturbing confidence.

End of Book I

*This is KNIT Powerscourt sh Cen
Constant Knitter . com.